Richard H. Triebe

i

PORT ROYAL

A novel
by
Richard H. Triebe

Smokey River Publishing
Wilmington, North Carolina

First published by Smokey River Publishing 10/20/2007

ISBN: 978-0-9798965-0-7

Printed in the United States of America

This book is printed on acid-free paper.

<u>Dedication</u>

This book would not have been possible without the help and support of my lovely wife Barbara Triebe. I love you Barbara for making me feel special everyday of my life. Without your encouragement *Port Royal* would still be a dream.

<u>Acknowledgements</u>

There are many people I would like to thank for editing my manuscript. Everyone had something unique to offer and you all helped make my story exceptional. I want to thank Wanda Canada, Carol Barre, Lonnie Holder, Christy Judah, Mac Moore, Jean Nance, Ellen Rickert and Barbara Triebe.

INTRODUCTION

Although this is a work of fiction, the facts on this page are true. In the latter 17th century, the town of Port Royal, Jamaica, became a den of pirates and thieves. The island of Jamaica was under loose British control after being taken from the Spanish in 1655. The British were constantly at war with Spain, and so, to help defend the island, they openly tolerated the presence of privateers. These privateers, or pirates, used the island as a fortress from which to attack the Spanish Fleets. Once they captured a Spanish ship, they would take it as a prize to Port Royal and sell the spoils. After the cargo was auctioned and the pirate crew had a little money to spend, they would begin their drunken carousing. Over 300 pirate crews called Port Royal home, and one out of every four buildings was either a tavern or a house of prostitution. Little wonder it became known as the "Wickedest City on Earth."

On June 7, 1692, a catastrophic earthquake caused the city to sink into the sea, killing more than three-quarters of its population. Over 2,500 people died and 1,800 buildings were destroyed. My story begins several days before that earthquake.

Except for historical references, the characters in this book are fictional. Any resemblance to any person, living or dead is purely coincidental.

Chapter 1

"Are you scared?" Amy asked. The nine-year-old's face appeared detached, unearthly. It floated out of the gloom, gaunt and questioning.

Jennifer did not answer.

Although it was nearly ten in the morning, their surroundings were as black and foreboding as a highwayman's cape at midnight. The girls sat on a dusty straw floor with their backs to a cool stone wall. The room was dark and its only light stabbed feebly around the slats of a small, boarded-up window. Now and then mysterious rustlings somewhere in the dark had the girls on edge.

Amy scooted forward and repeated the question, "Are you scared?"

Jennifer glanced away from her older sister. A fat tear raced down her cheek while the coarse texture of the rope burned into her wrists, holding them immobile.

"Don't be. Promise me you won't." Amy was near tears herself. "If you cry, I'll tell Papa!"

Jennifer swung around: her delicate doll-like cheeks were tear-streaked and angry. "Don't you dare!"

"I won't. I was only teasing."

Jennifer felt a little better now that Amy behaved like a normal sister. Sisters were meant to tease. That was typical. If Amy were ever nice, that would truly scare her. "No, I'm not scared. I know Papa will find us. And when he does—"

She was cut off by the piercing screech of stone attacking metal, a grinding wheel sound.

Both girls huddled closer. Amy stared at the door while Jennifer buried her face in the hollow of her older sister's shoulder and relived the nightmare. She wished they hadn't gone to gather okra and cassava that morning. She wished they hadn't left the house at all. That's when the hairy monster had grabbed them.

When the noise from the other room stopped, Jennifer looked up from her sister's shoulder and the movement made her wince.

"Do your hands hurt?" Amy asked.

Jennifer nodded.

"Mine, too. I've been trying to work them free, and I think I took some skin off."

Hearing about Amy's pains suddenly made hers worse. The rope seemed tighter and the burning more intense. "What do you think will happen?"

"They might bleed a little."

"No, you dummy, to us."

"I—I don't know," Amy faltered. She ignored the insult as if she hadn't heard it. Sisters could do that. They were allowed to call each other names. "I know if we don't get out of here soon, he'll be back."

"What'll we do?"

"Run away of course, but we've got to have a plan."

Both girls considered this. After a bit, Jennifer peered at her sister. Milky-white lines of concentration creased Amy's brow. She looked somehow older, wiser. Jennifer tried to imitate her sister. She stiffened her face and looked down at her torn and soiled dress. It was the flowered one her mother had spent so much time embroidering. Jennifer knew her mother would be furious about her ruined dress, but she would gladly accept any punishment her mother gave her if only they could be out of this awful place.

"I have it!" Amy cried. She was so delighted she almost shouted. "The door over there opens inward. We stand close to the wall, and when he opens it, we kick him in the shin and run."

"That's a plan?"

"Yes, I didn't have much to work with. There's nothing in this room but some old straw. We don't even have our hands free."

Jennifer frowned. "Some plan."

"If you don't like it, then you think of one."

"I will." She turned and studied the door. The more she thought about Amy's plan the better she liked it. It was simple enough to work, but it was missing something. They needed to keep the hairy monster from chasing after them until they could get away.

"I have it! We'll use your idea, but we've got to get these ropes off. We need to have our hands free so we can toss some sand into his eyes."

"I'm already working on mine, and they feel looser."

Jennifer wriggled her hands in the way only a seven-year-old can. In a minute she was free of her bonds. "Mine are off. Turn around so I can help you."

Amy's ropes untied easily. The two girls scooped up handfuls of sand from the straw floor and then crept close to the door. Amy Adamson took the lead because she was older. Now the terrible waiting began and the doubts started to creep in. Would the idea work? It seemed easy planning their escape, almost a game. Now it came dreadfully close to being a reality.

Amy hugged the wall. "Get ready," she whispered. "I think I hear him coming."

They tensed. Five minutes passed and still the door had not opened.

Jennifer relaxed. "I thought you said he was coming."

"No, I didn't. I said: I think."

Neither girl moved just in case, their faces intent, listening. A few more minutes went by.

"I don't think this was a very good idea," Jennifer said. "In fact, I think it stinks."

"Shh!"

She crinkled her face. "Oh, shush yourself. I'm not talking loud. Just because you're older doesn't mean you're smarter. You don't have all the brains, you know."

"Shhhhhhhh!"

Jennifer spoke quietly to herself. "I still think the idea stinks. It didn't have a chance anyw—"

The door burst open revealing swirling, smoke-gray dust in a brilliant shaft of light. A towering black figure appeared before them like an ominous dark cloud.

The girls threw their sand and darted out the door while the giant screamed in rage and pawed at his eyes, but not before Jennifer had gotten in a good swift kick.

*   *   *

The giant wiped the sand from his eyes and hammered the doorframe until the sharp cracking of splintering wood made him stop. The girls had gotten away. Matthew Hudson knew there was no use in chasing them. Not with his lame leg there wasn't. He limped to the front of his shop and removed the Meat Cutter sign. He was certain the girls would be back with others and maybe this diversion would create some confusion in locating his shop.

Matthew was a malignant scourge of a man. He stood six foot, four with crushing ape-like arms and wore flowing raven robes fastened by a brilliant scarlet sash. His massive head possessed a thick clot of greasy black hair with a wild tangle of beard to match. The most noticeable feature about him was his black, penetrating eyes. They were driving, evil eyes, the eyes of the devil himself.

He limped into the candle-lit room to the left. It was dark, the windows shuttered, just like the back room. Yellow light from thirteen tall candles jumped and flickered on the rough stone walls. The candles were pyramided on a blond hickory altar about five feet from a blood-red pillow that lay in the center of an eight-foot white circle within another circle. A pentagram stretched across its breadth pointing out a strange cryptic, Hebrew-like writing. One character appeared to be a note of music with a squiggly, tadpole tail; another looked like a comma; still another resembled a pipe standing on its stem; a fourth was a slithering snake and the last one did not resemble anything at all.

Matthew stepped into the middle of the circle, taking extreme care to avoid stepping on the sacred white lines, and knelt before the pillow. On it was cradled a silver ceremonial dagger with a goat's head handle. He picked up the dagger, held it out and bowed his head. "Oh, great Lucifer, the sacrificial virgin has escaped. If this humble servant is not worthy enough to serve you, then you may take my life instead."

The moving light made the blade appear to dance. Matthew grasped the handle with both hands, the tip of the blade toward his chest, and lifted his face. The knife seemed to take on a life of its own. It trembled as if under a great strain but did not come any closer to the man. When the quaking had ceased, Matthew brought the blade to his lips and kissed it. "Thank you, Lucifer. I'll bring you the girl. I swear it!"

Matthew bowed to the altar and stepped back from the circle. He pulled a black silken scarf from the bell of his right sleeve and carefully wrapped the knife. He then limped to the right of the doorway and counted seven stones up and three toward the corner. The stone he sought protruded slightly. With strong fingers he pulled it out and deposited the cloth-shrouded knife in the recess. From his front pocket, he took a scrap of Jennifer's dress, a lock of her hair, and a ball of twine and set these in there, also. He then replaced the stone. Matthew stepped to the side and spread a maroon and gold oriental carpet over the magic circle. For ten minutes he worked laboriously on his hands and knees, smoothing the carpet until he was satisfied it was free of wrinkles.

As Matthew thought of the girls, his anger began to mount, and his deep voice rose from a whisper to an insane shout. "There will be another time, another place. By all that I hold sacred, I swear it!"

*   *   *

The girls ran all the way home without daring to look back. Nearly a full kilometer to the north and west, home was a small, one and a half room dwelling with white Spanish walls and a weathered, gable roof. As usual, the door and windows were open allowing the light afternoon breeze to chase out the hot stuffy air.

Rose Marie Adamson sat at the wooden table mending the fuzzy, gray toe of a stocking that Ivor, her husband, had worn through. She was a young woman, only twenty-seven, but she appeared much older. Her dull brown hair, once gleaming chestnut, was tied haphazardly in a loose, droopy bun. Rose Marie's startling turquoise eyes gazed out at the world with practical frankness and saw it for what it was: hard work with little time for foolishness and rest. She was painfully thin, especially in the face, which was prematurely lined and seemed to record every hurt and indignity she had endured in her life.

When her daughters burst in the front door crying, Rose Marie dropped her mending and rushed to see what had happened. "Amy—Jennifer, what's wrong?"

"Mama, a big hairy monster is after us!" Jennifer said.

Rose Marie went to the door and glanced out. She saw no one and turned back to the girls.

"He's not, sweetheart. You're safe. Are either of you hurt?" She examined her children for any signs of injury.

"Yes, my wrists are burning!" Amy said, and held her hands out.

Rose Marie saw the skin was red and swollen. "Who did this?"

"The devil!" Jennifer blurted.

"He tied us up and was going to do something terrible to us! But we fooled him and ran away," Amy declared, looking proud.

"Yeah," Jennifer said, puffing out her chest. "We fooled him."

Rose Marie inspected the rope burns and shook her head. "Sit down, sweetheart, and don't touch those." She turned and Amy was no longer behind her. The girl had closed and locked the door and was peeking out the window. "Amy, come here."

Amy turned from the window trembling. "I'm afraid he's going to come here!"

Mrs. Adamson clasped her daughter to her bosom. "He won't. Your papa will see to that." She rocked her gently, and Jennifer came over and gave them both a hug. "Thank you, sweetheart. We needed that."

She got a bowl and filled it with water from a pitcher before returning to the table. "After I've taken care of these wrists we're going to the constable and report this."

"Are we going to have him arrested, Mama?" Amy asked, suddenly wide-eyed and hopeful, her face flushed with excitement; to a nine-year-old girl this was a daring adventure.

"Yes, we are. I know this isn't a decent place to raise children, but you girls should be safe, regardless." Rose Marie stopped and looked at them both, her thin face apologetic. "Your father and I—we're working very hard to move from here. It isn't easy. It costs lots of money." Rose Marie's eyes grew moist and she looked away.

Jennifer scooted off her chair and put a comforting arm around her mother. "Don't worry, Mama. We'll help, too."

"Thank you, sweetheart. I know you will." She hugged Jennifer, then Amy was there and she hugged her, too.

As Rose Marie and her daughters walked to the constable's office that afternoon, she was unsure she was doing the right thing.

She had always put the children's welfare first because she wanted them to have a better life than she had. Did she make the right decision?

The wagon-rutted street was heavy with dusty sunshine and excited wind-torn shouts. Gaily dressed peddlers in wide-brimmed straw hats were blustering at their donkeys, trying to coax a little more speed, as their drays careened through town on their way to the wharf. Five minutes earlier booming cannon had awakened the somnolent city and sent things into flight. It had alerted Port Royal to the approach of a triumphant privateer, and the drays would be needed to unload the booty. Even soldiers inside Fort Charles clustered at the nearest seaward parapet to watch the colorful procession. Well-dressed merchants closed their shops and joined the mob rushing to the waterfront to greet the vessel and to view the magnificent riches as they came ashore. After these were unloaded and tallied, they would be sold to the highest bidder. Then everyone would flock to the taverns for tankards of free-flowing rum, easy women and tales of daring piracy on the high seas.

"Why can't we tell papa what happened?" Jennifer moaned as if she were in great physical pain.

"Because we'd only upset him and the proper way, now that we have a constable, is to report it and let him take care of things." Rose Marie stooped before Jennifer. She wore a mob cap with the lappets tied under her chin and a green linen dress with a fitted bodice and a flared skirt. The cap made her narrow face look even thinner.

"You do understand, don't you?"

Still confused, Jennifer half-nodded, and then shook her head. She really didn't understand at all.

Her mother held her close and stared earnestly into her eyes. "I believe it's time you knew that your father has a violent temper."

Jennifer opened her mouth to protest, but her mother cut her off.

"It's true. You think your papa is a kind man. Well, he is, on the surface, but I'm afraid his temper may be the death of him yet."

Rose Marie cleared her throat and continued. "Back in London, when your papa was fourteen, he had a run-in with the law. The police were looking for a thief that fit your father's description. Ivor was helping his papa when a constable grabbed him. Your grandfather intervened and a fight broke out.

Unfortunately, both of them were beaten and put in jail. By evening your grandfather had become unconscious and twelve hours later, he died. When your Papa heard this, he went insane. He caused a riot in the prison and three jailers were injured. The court had no sympathy. They found him guilty of starting a riot, and they sentenced him to the penal colony in Jamaica. He has been very good since, but I'm afraid the news of your kidnapping may be too much for him. He might seek revenge and do something terrible, something the law could never forgive. Now do you understand why I don't want you to tell him?"

Jennifer met her mother's eyes and nodded.

"Good girl."

When traffic allowed they crossed the street. Even then they had to walk fast to dodge several drays. A huge, grinning Negro wearing a large gold earring pulled his wagon up smartly, tipped his hat, and allowed the girls to pass.

*   *   *

His brother-in-law had lied to him. "Go to Jamaica and become a rich man," he said. "I'll fix it for you," he said. Victor Chapman went to Jamaica through his brother-in-law's influence with King James, that much was true, but he had not become rich as promised. Not only was he separated from his wife, but the only position they could find for him was constable in the settlement at Port Royal. Constable? What did he know about the law? For that

8

matter, what did he know about being a constable in Jamaica? The only thing he knew was the town was full of cutthroats and thieves. He was afraid for his life every waking minute he spent in his office. This was why he spent as little time there as possible.

Victor pushed his chair from the long desk, picked up his ivory-headed walking stick and sauntered to the storeroom. He really didn't need the cane, but they were in vogue and every true gentleman possessed one.

Victor hoped his lavish clothes and portly build would show he was a man-of-means; that he was someone of incredible position and power who should be dealt with in the proper fashion. The low-crowned, wide-brimmed hat of Sicilian brown felt was trimmed with two orange-colored ostrich plumes. His periwig was loosely curled, cascading auburn tresses about his shoulders and collarless coat of heavy brick-red silk. He wore biscuit-colored silk stockings and breeches of brown velvet with gold loops at the knees. His sword hung loosely from a green silk baldric embroidered in gold and slung across his chest. It dangled like a useless toy as his ponderous belly pushed it forward and down.

Three smelly crates of salted fish, four bundles of sugarcane, two sacks of coconuts and seven stalks of bananas were the townspeople's dues for being allowed to operate, a friendly gift to the law. He would have several men take the fish to the meat cutter, but what should he do with the sugarcane, bananas and coconuts? He could not sell them. They were plentiful. Everyone could get all they wanted free. He shook his head and thought, *"This is a strange land with many wild and wonderful fruits. Why, the whole bloody island is practically a garden."*

At first Victor had greatly enjoyed the new fruit to be found here. There was nothing like them in England. Five months after his arrival, however, he had tired of their novelty. He already had them coming out of his ears and ass. They caused gas and he had the complaints something terrible. He brightened: Perhaps he would send them to his brother-in-law in England. A whole boatload! Victor chuckled at the thought of the fruit rotting and smelling up the wharf and worked out plans for it in his head. A bare-knuckled knock at the door broke his reverie.

Surely it was not a gentleman, Victor thought. *He would rap with his cane. Perhaps it was another peddler wishing to make a contribution.*

Constable Victor Chapman hurried to his desk, sat in the flame-red velvet chair and thrust his nose in the air to look more dignified. Dignity, after all, was everything.

"Come in." He looked and sounded totally bored.

The door opened slowly, almost hesitantly. Mrs. Adamson and her two girls stood at the threshold peeking cautiously in.

Chapter 2

Folding his robes gently Matthew Hudson put them under the hinged lid of the altar, then took a brass-bell snuff and put out the candles one-by-one. He loved the sweet, waxy scent of freshly extinguished candles almost as much as he loved the delicate fragrance of blood. The very thought of blood brought a smile to Matthew's face. *Blood felt good. It is so slippery, red and vital, especially between his fingers when it was still warm. To truly enjoy it he needed to immerse himself both physically and emotionally. Perhaps that's why I became a meat-cutter.*

Matthew picked up the oaken mallet, a fourteen-inch wooden handled knife, a worsted pouch and went to the back room. He crossed the room to open the shutters barring the windows. He shuffled along, the best he could, putting his good leg in front then drawing the shrunken one forward and along side. Walking this way was difficult, but he had learned to adapt rather well since his injury. He knew his limitations and accepted them without complaint. Some said Matthew was lucky to walk at all. Sometimes at night, especially when he had too much to drink, he would have dreams about what had happened before.

At fourteen Matthew was very large for his age; most people took him for four or five years older. He was a deck-hand on the merchant vessel *Wolf,* a brigantine of British registry. The master was Jonathan Thomas, a tough bantam-sized man, a few inches over five feet with unruly red hair that flowed into a thick, red beard. Captain Thomas was a seaman of the old school, harsh and tough with a temper to match. He tolerated no insubordination, idleness, or thievery among his crew. Woe is to the man who violated his rules.

One of Matthew's shipmates, an Irishman by the name of McDowell, had a pocket watch he admired. It was the most beautiful thing Matthew had ever seen: golden yellow with an elegant three-masted sailing ship on the front of the case. Not like the clumsy merchantman he was on, but a well fitted-out, handsome craft the likes of which made him daydream of being a romantic seaman and traveling to far off, exotic lands. When McDowell held it in his fingers and rocked it back and forth it would cease to be an engraving. Matthew could really see it sail, its canvas full to bursting and running before the wind. McDowell would watch Matthew, then grin crookedly with that way he had and say, *It caught a wee bit'o magic when it was made, Laddie. If'n ya truly believe, it'll take yer soul and sail forever.*

Matthew was excited, captivated. He knew he must have the watch. He needed it. One night, when they were approaching the West Indies from the south and McDowell was sleeping off the effects of too much rum, Matthew sneaked below and crept to the man's hammock. He found seaman as he had expected, snoring and dead to the world. Matthew knew he kept the watch in the left front pocket of his breeches. With stealth, he slipped in his fingers and gently probed for the case, but McDowell woke and saw him. At first the Irishman looked confused, as if he might be having a dream. Then he grabbed Matthew's hand and started yelling.

Matthew carried a Billy club in his waistband and beat McDowell repeatedly about the head and shoulders with it. McDowell's nose blossomed like a red gurgling rose, his mouth turned to soft crimson mush and his hands fell away.

Matthew clutched the watch and bolted up the stairs. Freedom, starlight and fresh breezes waited above. As he was about to clear the last two steps something grabbed his foot. He looked down and saw a horrible apparition that resembled McDowell. The hideous smear of his mouth was vermilion and dripping; it hung loosely open with no teeth. His eyes were staring and his nose was an oozing open wound.

Matthew tried to jerk his foot away, but the gore-spattered man possessed the strength of a demon. McDowell's mouth was flapping grotesquely, his tongue a fat livid worm. He reached out for Matthew, climbing the steps two at a time.

Matthew planted his foot firmly on the top step and kicked wildly with the free one. He bashed the red slippery face below the left eye and then caught the side of the head and his throat. The effect was devastating. When the square-toed boot struck the soft flesh Matthew heard a sickening snap. McDowell gazed with disbelief, then turned to instant deadweight and fell to the floor with a broken neck.

Matthew swung around and saw Captain Thomas glaring at him through dark, malevolent eyes. If he hated thieves, he hated murderers even more. The captain drew a pistol from his jacket (he was always armed to enforce his law) and started across the deck. His lips were working, but Matthew could only hear a distant muffled sound. Matthew spun around, snatched up a wooden hatch cover and ran to the railing. He flung the cover to the black water below and dove after it. The captain's pistol exploded and shattered Matthew's leg as he left the ship.

Matthew was incapable of swimming for more than a few minutes and would surely drown. He remembered what McDowell had said about the watch: "It caught a wee bit'o magic when it was made, Laddie. If'n ya truly believe, it'll take yer soul and sail forever."

Matthew clutched the watch and wished with all of his might to be saved. He wished so hard the blood rushing to his temples made him light-headed, and he nearly blacked out. That is when he bumped into the hatch cover and pulled himself aboard. Finding it had been a miracle! Matthew gazed at the golden watch in his hand and wondered if it really could save him.

After many hours, Matthew washed ashore on the southwest corner of St. Lucia. A strange little man by the name of George Lightfoot discovered him and took him in. George was a very handsome man: half-Indian with dark eyes and a proud nose. His hair was straight and black as a dense thicket of spruce at midnight, and velvety bronze skin softened his angular features.

Because he delved in magic for no personal gain George was considered a white witch. He merely liked to help others less fortunate. If you were a fisherman, you went to George and asked his blessing before you would cast your net; if you were a farmer you went to him before planting a seed; the hunter, the baker and the shipbuilder all did the same. They would walk from surrounding villages and take him a gift, some food perhaps, and ask if God smiled upon them. Usually George would answer favorably, and they would beam and nod their heads. He would bless them anyway, even if they didn't need his help, because it was mostly reassurance they sought. Other times, when he saw dark clouds on their horizon, he would do much more. These people were the ones who needed his help the most. He would chant from inside a magic circle drawn in the dirt, scatter personal possessions of the people he wished to help (bits of the person's hair or fingernails) along with a mysterious white powder he kept in a small leather pouch, and they never failed to have a bountiful year.

When Matthew was healthy again and first saw this, he was puzzled. He asked the old man why he did not use the power for himself.

"Because it is a gift," George had answered. "If you use this force only for yourself it will soon turn against you, and there is no magic in the world that can ease your suffering."

"Suffering? What suffering? The only suffering I can see is caused by this rundown shack we're living in and the tattered rags on our backs."

The old man gazed at him for a moment and shook his head in disgust. "It's not good to speak of such things. To even think them. There's no need of it."

"You have such power! Just think of all the riches you could have. You wouldn't have to live in this dirty, rundown shack, practically begging for your supper. Kings would come to you, their hats in their hands. They would bow and offer you anything in their kingdom: Gold, jewels, the prettiest wenches, their own daughters even."

George spun around, his dark eyes venomous. For a fearful moment Matthew thought he might strike him. "Don't say such things! You don't know what it can do. The power can turn black and sour."

George was right of course. The youth did not understand.

Matthew saw the anger on the old man's face and wisely said no more.

Before the year was out Matthew had become apprenticed to George and did most of the menial chores, which were numerous. Sometimes Matthew thought George dreamed up new tasks for him to do just to keep him out of trouble. However, the long hours of toil would pay their dividends when George would show him a new trick or a bit of magic. Oh, there was some trickery to be sure. But the meat of the show, the very heart, was pure magic.

Matthew was delighted. He was learning a skill, a craft to be respected, even feared. *Someday*, he thought, *I, not George, will be the lord of the manor. I will reap the benefits and do as I please without the weakling George to interfere.* Meanwhile, he would do as he was told and learn as much as he could.

It happened by accident at first, quite innocently in fact. A fisherman by the name of Nesbit had come with his son to receive George's blessing for a good catch. As usual, George had taken a lock of hair from each of their heads, spread it around the magic circle and did his curious chanting dance. Matthew waited until everyone had left, picked up the scattered hair and conjured up some magic of his own: black magic. He believed his pocket watch possessed magic powers, so he placed it in the center of the circle to help focus his psychic energy. Matthew didn't really expect the curse to work. It was almost certain not to. But work it did—with frightening vengeance.

Nesbit had gone out on his sloop, the *Mary-Ann*, with his son and another man. Not only did they not catch a single fish, but Nesbit's only son had fallen overboard and was eaten by a large shark that had been shadowing the boat all day. His friend restrained the distraught man from throwing himself into the water to save his son.

The next time Matthew tried out his powers was less than a week later. Six people had come to see George: A glowing bride to be, the happy groom and their smiling parents. They wanted to wish the new couple well so they might have a long, happy marriage with many healthy children.

George took a ceremonial clipping from everyone and went into his special marriage circle. He had the bride and groom step in, too. They held hands while he spread the hair about and chanted in some strange tongue. When he was through the delirious couple and their elated parents pumped George's hand profusely and went home to prepare for a magnificent wedding.

Matthew crept from hiding, gathered the hair from the ground and made his own magic circle. With the aid of the watch he conjured up the most evil, foul curse to ever be put upon a young couple. Matthew was not doing this to be malicious. He just wanted to prove to himself that the first time was no accident, that he really possessed the power. They were married two days later. Inside a week the bride had fallen sick with an unknown illness and died. Grief stricken, the groom had committed suicide by hanging himself from the rafters of their new honeymoon house.

The day following the man's funeral Matthew was out gathering firewood for the smokehouse. He had found as much as he could safely carry on his back and decided to head for home. A loud commotion stopped Matthew as he reached the trees at the edge of the clearing near his house. An angry mob was in front of the house brandishing sticks and hurling stones. Matthew looked for George but couldn't find him. *Perhaps he fled out the back,* he thought. To Matthew's horror, he saw the old man hadn't. Four people, one was Nesbit another was the late bride's father, carried the struggling little man on their shoulders. He was bleeding from the nose and forehead, his hair wildly askew. The crowd buzzed even louder when they saw him and a few chanted, "Kill him! Kill him! Kill him!" Soon everyone picked up the cry and the whole clearing rang with, **"Kill him! Kill him! Kill him!"**

The men carried George to a stout tree. He was crying and pleading with them to stop, that he hadn't done anything wrong. His begging just seemed to fuel the ugly fire of hate. He pleaded with them to let him go when a rope appeared and flew around the tree's trunk.

A large man with a billowing sandy beard quickly tied George to the tree while the crowd piled branches around its base. George swung his head feverishly as a gag was shoved into his mouth and someone tossed a flaming torch onto the wood.

A hush fell over the crowd as wispy tendrils of blue-gray smoke curled around the bound and gagged figure. The orange flames spread quickly in the dry wood and roared up the struggling man, cycloning burning embers into the air.

Matthew refused to watch anymore. He realized he couldn't come out of hiding or they might burn him also. Visibly shaken, he slipped quietly into the woods.

Matthew managed to stay away three days before he got so hungry that he had to go back. He knew a hindquarter of ham was in the smokehouse and that it was most likely untouched because the shack laid several hundred feet behind the house. George had insisted it be far enough from their home to keep the smoke away no matter which way the wind blew. If he were lucky, he might find some bread or cheese to go with the meat.

Matthew crept near the clearing and watched the house and surroundings for over an hour to make sure it was deserted. Finally, he sneaked into the clearing and eyed the macabre form: half-man, half-blackened bone. The breeze wafted the sickening smell of charred flesh in his direction. George had lost his gag and his mouth was open in a silent scream. The skin from his forehead and cheeks hung in black, curling strips and his eyes were gone. The lower body had two blackened stumps of bone, but no feet, clothing or flesh at all. Matthew's knees grew weak and buckled. He had to forcefully shut his mouth and look away to keep from vomiting.

Matthew found the ham, but the cupboard held no food, only a few battered pewter bowls and mugs. He carried his booty back to the woods, but he did not eat ravenously as he had expected. Several hours later, when his stomach allowed, Matthew ate modestly while planning his revenge.

His plan was simple. Matthew had possessed it in his subconscious all along. He did not need people to come to him to work his magic, not as long as he had some fingernail clippings or some hair from the victims. Matthew went back to the clearing and searched the ground within the magic circles. It took him over two hours, but he had finally found enough personal effects of the villagers to perform the necessary rites. These few items, along with his watch, were all Matthew needed.

Nesbit's boat sank in a matter of days, taking three men from the village with it. One night the parents of the bride and groom had their homes burn to the ground, killing three of them. The fourth, the bride's mother, went crazy. A drought came and all of the livestock in the area died. Soon the village, like the crops, just withered and blew away. With all the bad luck, people refused to live there anymore, figuring the land was bewitched.

His work done, Matthew walked to Soufrie're and booked passage on a ship bound for Jamaica where he would be unknown. In 1687, he settled in Port Royal and became a meat-cutter.

Chapter 3

Mrs. Adamson stood at the threshold with her two girls, not knowing whether to step inside. She had come this far, she reasoned, why not go a little further?

She took several halting steps, and stopped just inside the door. The girls were all eyes, clinging to her skirt. In the center of the room was a large imposing stretcher-based desk with huge ball feet. Behind it sat a corpulent gentleman wearing a brown felt hat trimmed with two orange ostrich plumes.

"Excuse me, sir. Are you the constable?"

The gentleman looked up from a piece of parchment he was studying, his face and voice impeccably bored. "I am. Who might you be?"

"My name is Mrs. Ivor Adamson and I wish to report the attempted kidnapping of my two daughters."

Victor Chapman pointed a chubby pink finger adorned with a massive gold ring that had a claret red stone. He wiggled it impatiently. "These are the girls?"

"Yes, Amy and Jennifer." Jennifer peeked out from behind her mother's flowing green skirt. Rose Marie grasped her daughter by the shoulder and nudged her forward.

"Well, young lady," the constable said, "suppose you tell me what happened?"

Jennifer's eyes were big, and she had tucked her chin in as far as it would go. She remained silent, staring.

Victor looked at her mother. "The child can talk, can't she?"

Rose Marie nodded. "Jennifer, tell the nice man what he wants to know."

When her sister didn't answer Amy broke in impatiently, "What about me? I was there too."

Victor turned to her. "All right then, why don't you tell me what happened?"

"My sister and I went to gather cassava root near the salt marshes. When we went between the tavern and the ship chandlers a big hairy man grabbed us. He was—"

"The devil!" Jennifer said in a rush.

All eyes turned to her. Her face colored and she exclaimed, "Well, he was!"

The constable gave her mother an exasperated look. He asked Amy, "Which tavern?"

Amy fidgeted and thought a moment.

Jennifer spoke again, quickly and with determination. "The Blue Dolphin Inn. It's between Landstrom's Ship Chandlers and the blacksmith's."

The constable nodded, his orange plumes jerking wildly, amplifying the man's movements. "Yes, go on."

"The man stepped out in front of us when we turned the corner near the tavern. He grabbed us before we could run away."

"What did he do then?"

"He carried us away."

"Aha! Then he had a partner."

"No, he didn't," Jennifer said.

Victor chortled confused, "I don't understand? How could one man do all of the things you describe?" The constable's eyes narrowed, his features stern. "Are you sure that's how it happened? Come now, tell me the truth."

"I am!" Jennifer cried, her eyes clouded over and her cheeks began to quiver. She looked to her mother, but Rose Marie was too busy glaring at the constable to notice her. Fire flashed in the woman's eyes. "Please don't torment my daughter any further! Can't you see she's trying to remember?"

The constable motioned to the papers on the desk. "My dear lady, as you can see I'm a busy man. Do you wish to report this and catch the man or not?"

"Of course we do! Otherwise, we wouldn't be here."

"Then let me ask my questions. I'm trying to ferret out the truth."

"How? By frightening a child senseless?"

Victor glared at her, the color rushing to his face. "Shall I continue?"

"Of course I want you to continue, but please do not grill her as if she were the criminal."

The constable looked at the girls. "Jennifer, you too, Amy, let me see if I have the story right. You were going to gather cassava this morning, and you were walking between the Blue Dolphin Inn and the ship chandlers when this man grabbed you."

Both girls nodded.

"Good! Can you describe him for me?"

"He was a big man with a beard and dressed in black," Amy began. "Then he picked us up and put his hands over our mouths."

"A big smelly hand!" Jennifer blurted.

The constable ignored her and continued staring at Amy. "He picked both of you up simultaneously?"

"Yes."

"Extraordinary. Where did he take you?"

"To a white building not far from here."

"Do you think you could find it again?"

"Yes, I think so. It had an awful sign in front. It was a picture of a slaughtered pig strung up by his feet and dripping blood into a bucket."

Victor knew the sign she described. "What did the sign say?"

"I don't know." Amy looked down self-consciously. "I can't read."

The constable nodded in appreciation. "What did he do then? Took you inside, I presume?"

"Yes, he tied us up," Amy said.

Jennifer, eyes solemn but proud, held out her bandaged wrists as evidence.

"Then he did something strange, I thought. He cut some of my sister's hair and took a piece of her dress, then put us in a dark smelly room in the back. We managed to escape when he opened the door."

"I see," Victor said to the girls and then glanced at their mother. "May I speak with you in private, Mrs. Adamson?"

"Of course."

The constable turned to the girls again. "Thank you for bringing this to my attention. What you've done was very brave, and we should reward both of you."

The girls smiled, pleased with themselves.

"Are either of you hungry?"

The sisters looked at each other and then turned expectantly to their mother.

"It's all right. Just be careful not to spoil your supper."

Amy nodded eagerly, but Jennifer, being her normal reserved self, did not.

"Good," the constable said, his face jovial. "I have some delightful bananas in the back. If you go through that door, you'll find several bunches."

The girls were reluctant to leave their mother and stayed put.

"Go on—go!" He shooed them with both hands, causing his ruffled cuffs to flutter. Victor followed them with amused eyes as they disappeared into the back. "Eat as many as you can," he called. "Then I'll see who the winner is."

He rose and shut the door behind them, then slid the barrel bolt home. A new Victor Chapman turned around; the smile had changed from one of fatherly benevolence to an intimidating leer. He walked over to Rose Marie, taking off his jacket. "Take your clothes off. We haven't much time."

"What are you saying?" Rose Marie asked, indignant.

"I'm saying that Matthew Hudson paid you fifty gold sovereigns for your daughters, and I feel I deserve something for my cooperation in your scheme."

"Are you crazy?"

"Oh, come now. Don't play innocent with me. Mr. Hudson came to me right after your girls escaped and told me all about it."

"What do you mean?"

"You know very well what I mean. He warned me you might reconsider and come here to report him."

Victor plucked a frilly, rose-colored hanky from his cuff and dabbed at his moist upper-lip before continuing.

"Matthew said he paid you fifty gold sovereigns, so I know you have enough to share with the local constable to guarantee his silence."

Rose Marie's arms were ramrod straight, and her hands were balled into fists of white-knuckled rage. She had been found out, but she remained defiant. "I don't have the money," she spat. "I spent it."

Victor Chapman laughed. "Oh, really? You couldn't possibly have spent it in so short a time. Besides, if you did you'd have nothing with which to bargain. You don't have your children anymore. I have them." The constable walked to the front door and slid the bolt home. "In fact, I also have you. Shall we bargain for your life? Say . . . fifty pieces of gold?"

"I can't! I don't have it."

"How much do you have?"

"I can give you ten gold sovereigns."

"That's not what I asked. I said: How much do you have?"

She glared at him. "Twenty-five pieces of gold."

"Where is the rest?"

"I've hidden the money at home. It's for my husband and me. I'll give it to you. All fifty pieces if you'll just let me and the girls go."

Victor shook his head. "Enough of this dickering. We haven't much time. Mr. Hudson will be here shortly."

"I'll give you the money if you let me go—not the girls. Mr. Hudson said he wouldn't hurt them. He said there are rich families who would be willing to pay for healthy children."

"All right," Victor said, his face came alive, especially the eyes. They sparkled with glee. "I'll let you go and say nothing about your involvement if you bring me the gold this afternoon. Not all of it, mind you. I want to keep you happy. Say . . . twenty-five gold sovereigns and your virtue?"

Rose Marie's chest heaved with barely controllable rage. The thought of having sex with the fat, piggish man turned her stomach.

"Agreed!" she hissed.

The constable leered at her with new appreciation and opened the door. "Remember, I want you and the gold here this afternoon, otherwise I'll tell everything I know."

"Don't worry. I'll remember," Rose Marie said, forcing a smile of defiance.

The storeroom in the constable's office had red brick walls and only one high narrow window.

Jennifer grabbed Amy by the arm and whispered, "The constable scares me. I don't trust him."

"Why?"

"I don't know," she said with a puzzled voice. "I just don't."

"You're an old fraidy-cat."

"I am not!"

"You are so. When he was questioning you, you were so scared I thought you were going to wet your pants."

Jennifer appeared hurt because it was nearly true. "That's not funny," she said. Then trying to change the subject, she spied the yellow-green bananas. "Neither is this fruit. It looks yucky!"

"It is not. They're just bananas."

"It is so. I don't like to eat anything green." Jennifer wrinkled her nose, proving her enormous distaste. "It might be slimy." Her nose wrinkled even more. "And what is that awful smell?"

The girls looked and found three crates of salted fish under the bananas.

"Oh, double yucky!" Jennifer cried. "Let's get out of here!"

"We can't. Mama and Mr. Chapman are still talking. They sent us back here so they could be alone."

Amy surveyed the tiny room, and her gaze finally returned to the stalks of bananas. She broke off two of the riper ones and handed the fruit to her sister. "Here, try one. They must be good to eat because I've seen them growing on that new plantation."

Jennifer must have forgotten about it being yucky for she examined it closely, feeling it all over. She bit into the stem and frowned. "I don't know. It's very stringy."

Amy laughed. "You've got to peel it first, you idiot."

Jennifer spat the stem into her hand and made a face. It was all green and wet and looked like a squashed caterpillar. "I knew that."

Amy took a healthy bite, and her cheeks blew up like a fat squirrel's.

Jennifer laughed hysterically.

Amy stopped chewing. "What's so funny?"

"You are, dopey. You make the funniest faces when you eat." She puffed out her cheeks and they began laughing. The girls had the giggles and they were so hard to stop once they started.

Ten minutes later, after they had eaten two bananas each, they were full to bursting and feeling more than a little restless.

"I can't eat another bite," Jennifer said, holding her stomach, her face pale. "Do you think mama's through yet?"

Amy went to the door and put her ear against it. "I don't know. I can't hear anything." She tried opening it. The brass handle turned, but the door would not budge. "It's locked!" Amy screamed, her eyes registering total shock.

"Are you sure?"

Amy tried again and nodded. Her eyes had a glazed terrified look.

Jennifer went to the door and tried the knob. When it would not open, she beat on the door, tears streaming down her cheeks. "Please, Mama, open up! It's me, Jennifer!" She continued pounding until her hands grew sore, then stopped to listen. There wasn't a sound except Amy weeping softly behind her.

"Mama, pleeeaaassseee!" Jennifer wailed, crimson faced.
Amy joined her sister at the door and both cried and pounded in unison. "Mama! Maaammmmmmaaaaaaaaa!"

Through watery eyes Amy spied the small window. "Jennifer, look! There's a window. Help me stack these crates so I can get up there."

Each crate was two feet high so they stacked all three, two on the bottom, one on the top, like a set of stairs.

Amy scrambled to the top, but to her dismay she found rusting iron bars outside the window. They were spaced six inches apart and presented a formidable barrier. The bars were designed to keep adults out, she reasoned, not children. She pulled the dress over her head.

Jennifer gawked at Amy clad only in linen underwear. "What are you doing?"

"Taking this dress off. I can probably slip through these iron bars without this."

Amy grabbed a bar in either hand and tried to squeeze her head through. The bars were a bit too close, so the girls were back to where they had started.

Jennifer tore her dress off and began rubbing her face and hair with banana peels. "Get down and let me try," she ordered.

Amy climbed down and watched her sister scale the boxes. Jennifer's sack-like linen undergarment flapped wildly as her muscles worked. She gained the top and rubbed the bars with banana skins until they were black and shiny with the sweet smelling oil. She grabbed them and managed to slip her head through. The bars pulled at her ears, but she turned sideways and pulled herself along. In a moment, she was through and sitting on the ledge on the other side.

"Now you," Jennifer whispered as she clung to the bars like a monkey. "Do as I did. Grease yourself really well, and I'll meet you outside." Without another word, she let go and dropped from view.

Amy did as her sister had suggested. When she was greasy, she picked up both dresses and climbed to the top of the crates. Amy turned her head as she heard deep voices in the next room. With renewed terror, she faced the window and slipped the dresses through. The voices were much louder, more angry. She must hurry! Amy climbed onto the ledge, grabbed the bars and tried to force her head through. Unfortunately, she met more resistance than Jennifer. The brawling voices became thunderous. She tried again to push through the bars, but they seemed just as cold and forbidding as before. She closed her eyes, pushed extra hard, and willed herself through. It worked! She was sliding through easily now. In a few seconds she joined Jennifer on the ground.

"I heard voices," Amy said. "Men's voices."

She took Jennifer's hand and sneaked to the corner window of the constable's office. The diamond-quarreled glass was dusty and hard to see through, but if it was shaded just right it was possible to see Matthew Hudson and the constable.

The bearded giant's voice boomed as he gestured wildly a few inches from the other man's face, "Where are they?"

"That's him!" Jennifer exclaimed, her eyes doubly round.

"That's the man who kidnapped us!"

"Shhhh!" Amy whispered. She pulled her sister away from the window, so the two men would not see them.

"Where is mama?" Jennifer asked.

"I don't know. Maybe they tied her up."

Amy was silent, thinking. Finally, she said, "We've got to tell Papa. He'll know what to do."

Jennifer eagerly nodded and followed her sister. When the street was clear, they ran across it clutching their gaily-flowered dresses in their hands, their cream-colored undergarments flapping in the breeze.

*   *   *

If Matthew Hudson appeared evil when he was at peace, now he seemed murderous.

"You fool!" he boomed in a voice so deep and chilling it seemed to echo from the bowels of hell. "Why did you let her go? She'll tell everyone."

Victor Chapman backed away from the violent and crazy man who towered over him like a dark menacing cloud. "She'll come back. She said she would. Besides, I have something better than her word. I have her children."

Matthew scanned the room. "Where?"

"In—in the back," Victor stammered, pointing a trembling finger, his heavy gold ring doing a jig.

Matthew shoved the constable toward the back room. Victor Chapman crashed into the door. With nervous fingers, he fumbled with the bolt and opened it. Matthew flung him into the room. Victor slammed into the wall, losing his plumed hat and knocking his periwig cockeyed.

"Where are they?"

"I—I don't know. They—they were here a minute ago."

The open window was as obvious as a red flag to both men.

Matthew Hudson's gaze was cold as steel. "You bumbling fool! You had all three in your grasp and you let them slip through your fat greedy fingers." He approached the quivering man with slow, deliberate steps. "Letting you live seems to be a luxury I can ill afford."

Victor had nowhere to go but against the wall behind him. Despite his enormous size, Matthew Hudson was on him in an instant, his ponderous weight pinning the smaller man and rendering him helpless. The constable's sword was useless as always. His arm didn't have the elbow room necessary to draw it from its scabbard.

Victor was aware of Hudson's huge twisting hands on his head right before his neck snapped. He dropped to the floor amid a yellow field of sweet smelling banana peels, his glassy eyes staring at the ceiling.

Chapter 4

Ivor Noel Adamson inspected the gaping crack in the ship's side from the scaffold. It was so large, almost one half inch, that if it was not for the double hull he would see daylight. Two weeks over thirty years, eleven of those years working for the Landstrom Shipyard, Ivor was the master-carpenter he had always hoped he would be. His twinkling green eyes beneath his bobbed wheat-colored hair gleamed with an intensity that never seemed to dim despite his mood. He dragged the back of his hand across his sweating brow and reexamined the crack. A rivulet of salty liquid ran down his prominent cheekbones and settled into the corner of his mouth, the mouth that made him devilishly handsome when he smiled. He wasn't smiling now. As he picked up the proper width of oakum his tawny, nankeen breeches stretched above hazel stockings. His cream-colored cotton shirt was open at the collar, while its neck cloth hung loosely to the side. Ivor shoved the sticky, black hemp into the crack and inspected it before pounding it in place with a wooden mallet. If he had told Rogers once, he had told him a thousand times to get the planks closer together. Someday a ship might be in serious danger if he allowed this shoddy work to continue.

Ivor went down the line shoving oakum into the crack until it ran its course and became narrow again. He only wished he could solve his problems at home as easily as mending the cracks in the hull.

Business had been very slow, and the shipyard had to cut back. That meant fewer hours for Ivor. His wife, Rose Marie, had been irritable lately. He could understand her anger, what with the pressures of trying to run a household on too little money, but he could not see why she directed her anger at their daughters when he alone was responsible.

Ivor straightened up, placed a hand in the small of his back, and stretched. His stomach was on fire and seemed as if it wanted to burn itself up. The pressures were getting to him as well. These thoughts had him believing his wife was a changed woman, that she didn't really love her children. The idea was ridiculous. Whoever heard of a woman who didn't adore her children? Ivor felt ashamed for thinking such thoughts. Work was distorting things, making him crazy. Rose Marie was the stabilizing force that held the family together.

Ivor decided to buy her something frivolous to brighten her mood, something she would never buy herself. Perhaps he might get the set of tortoiseshell combs she had admired so much. He would talk to Bjorn, the owner of the shipyard, and see if he could get an advance on his pay and maybe get off work early.

Ivor jumped off the scaffold and clapped Rogers on the back. The giant merely stared after him, as Ivor, with a spring in his step, headed for the red tile and stone building near the street.

*   *   *

The girls ran under a delicately arched sign that read: "LANDSTROM'S SHIPYARD AND CAREENING PEN." They failed to find their father on one of the scaffolds so they went to the yard office. It was a small, gray stone building with a red, terra-cotta tile roof. Like most of the buildings in Port Royal, it consisted of stone that had once been used as ship's ballast.

Amy stepped through the door holding Jennifer's hand and clutching her dress. The office's furniture consisted of a badly scarred table and two equally battered chairs. Behind the table, leaning back in a chair and puffing on a slender, white clay pipe was Bjorn Landstrom. He was a big, outdoor-hardened man with laughing cobalt-blue eyes beneath an uncontrolled mane of flaxen hair. He took small puffs from the pipe and spoke in a heavy Nordic accent.

"What do we have here? Two lost girls in their nightshirts . . . or maybe you're applyin' for a job." Due to his thick accent, job sounded like yob.

"No, sir," Amy said, bunching the material of her linen shift nervously. "We're looking for our Papa, Ivor Adamson. We can't find him anywhere."

"Ivor? You're Ivor's little girls?" Landstrom regarded them both, and then wrinkled his nose, sniffing the air around him. "That's funny. It smells jus' like bananas in here." He glanced at his pipe and sniffed it, suspiciously.

The girls giggled.

"Yes, Ivor," Landstrom continued. "I let him go early. Said he had an errand to run."

"Please, sir," Amy said, "it's very important we find papa right away."

Landstrom leaned forward, placing two beefy arms on the table. He drew the pipe from his mouth. "Maybe I can help. Why don't you tell me what the trouble is?"

"Well, our mother is missing. We think the same man who took us has her."

"Someone tried to kidnap you?"

The girls nodded.

Bjorn clapped his desk with a huge callused hand. It boomed like thunder, and the girls were taken aback with fear and awe. "It's a good thing you came to me then. I'll do everything I can to help."

He rose to his feet and walked over to the girls. Like magic, the pipe found his mouth again and ringed his head in smoke. "Come along," he said, taking each by the hand with his big mitts.

Outside they found Big John Rogers, biceps bulging, hammering large iron spikes through oak planks into massive wooden ribs. Landstrom left the girls to talk to the giant alone.

They spoke quietly. Rogers nodded to Landstrom, and then looked at the girls. He dropped his hammer and the two men walked over.

Amy nodded politely, but Jennifer was gawking wide-eyed at Big John. To a small girl he looked as huge as a mountain and twice as awesome. In reality, he was six foot eight, but from her vantage point he seemed to touch the sky. His bare chest was a sea rippling with sun-bronzed muscles. Instead of the customary knee breeches, he wore baggy brown pants that stopped short of his ankle a full six inches. Jennifer figured the shortness of his pants was either to keep him cool while he worked or maybe, and she thought this highly probable, they didn't make pants large enough to fit him.

Big John walked over to the girls and offered a huge hand to each of them.

"Don't worry, little ones, I will not let anyone hurt you. Come on, we're going home."

*　　*　　*

Matthew Hudson peered through the crude, uneven glass at the surrealistic image of Rose Marie Adamson. She sat at the kitchen table holding her head in her hands, weeping. Matthew found the door locked, so he kicked it in.

Rose Marie shot bolt-upright, her eyes fearful.

Storming into the room Matthew flung the table aside with a swipe of his huge hand. The table crashed into the brick wall and fell to the floor in pieces. With his other hand he grabbed Rose Marie and dragged her toward the door. She became a screaming wildcat, beating on his chest and raking his face with her fingernails. Matthew had enough of this insolent woman. Drawing back his fist, he struck Rose Marie on the chin, knocking her unconscious.

Matthew threw Rose Marie on the bed, wrapped her in a gray blanket and hefted the bundle to his shoulder. Even though the blanket flopped open revealing the woman inside, Matthew didn't care. He knew everyone in town minded their own business. Throughout the years Port Royal had earned its reputation as "The Wickedest City on Earth", and no one with any sense would dare to stop him, not even the soldiers. He used the term soldiers lightly, because the British soldiers were a local joke. They rarely ventured outside Fort Charles and when they did, they traveled in groups. Matthew squared his shoulders, put a steadying hand on the bundle, and went through the shattered doorway.

*   *   *

When Big John saw the Adamson's door torn off its hinges he motioned for the girls to stay back.

"You girls stay here while I go inside and look around."

The girls nodded and held hands while Big John disappeared through the splintered doorway. He returned in a moment to motion that it was safe to enter.

Big John did not say much. He did not have to. The girls could see someone had been there, wrecked the house, and probably kidnapped their mother. He was gone now and it was safe with Big John there, but a distinct feeling of dread permeated everything.

Jennifer sat quietly in a chair, the handsome banister-backed one her mother was so fond of, and tearfully eyed the broken table against the wall. Amy, acting incredibly grown-up, tried to keep busy so she would not cry, too. She got some kindling from the chest by the hearth and some wood from outside. In a minute she had a small, but hopeful fire burning and hung a kettle of water from the wrought-iron hanger for tea.

Big John wanted to find their mother, but he wouldn't leave the girls alone. He studied the door's splintered edge to see if he could rehang it. Occasionally he would sneak glances at Amy and Jennifer and his eyes would grow moist. Mostly he watched Jennifer sit in her mother's chair staring at the table. A bond grew between them. Big John had no children, and he began to feel fatherly toward her. He leaned the door against the wall and went to work on the shattered table. He fit the pieces together as best he could and soon set a crooked, but sturdy, table before the young girl.

She looked up and tried to smile a thank you, but it did not come off as intended. Her smile was anemic and withered a second after it started. Big John's heart went out to the sad youngster. He wished he could go out and find her mother to make the girl happy again, but he could not leave the sisters alone. Instead, he busied himself repairing the door and got it rehung by the time Ivor and Bjorn hurried in.

"What happened?" Ivor asked.

"Your wife's gone. Someone broke in, and there's sign of a struggle," Big John said.

Jennifer ran to her father and cried, "Papa, someone took Mama! I think it was that man who tried to steal us this morning."

"What man? Can you show me where he is?"

"Yes, I think so."

The four of them searched for the building where the girls were held captive. The girls pointed out a building, but the doors and windows were locked.

Ivor beat on the front door demanding, "Open up! I know you've got my wife in there!"

After several minutes, Big John stepped forward and asked, "Would you like me to break down the door?"

Ivor thought a moment. He wanted to get inside and find his wife, but what if this were the wrong building? Children often make mistakes. "No. I want to be certain we have the right place." He turned to the girls and asked, "You're sure this is where he took you?"

The girls looked at the front of the shop. The awful sign they had seen before was gone.

"I think it is, but the sign is missing," Jennifer said.

"How about you, Amy? Are you sure?"

"I'm not certain, but I'm pretty sure."

"Girls, I have to know if this is the building. Otherwise, we could be damaging someone else's property."

Amy shrugged her shoulders. "I guess I'm not so sure anymore."

Ivor turned to Big John. "John, would you take the girls home while Bjorn and I go to the shipyard and organize a search party?"

"Sure. They'll be safe with me. You just go and find your wife."

The men searched the streets and the woods near town until late, but failed to find any trace of his wife.

After Big John and the girls returned home, he got them ready for bed. Amy and Jennifer slipped into their flowered nightshirts and crawled into their "William and Mary" style double bed. Big John stretched out on the floor near the foot of the bed, so effectively that his body barred any access to the sleeping girls.

Jennifer saw the big man lie down, took a patchwork quilt from the bed, and covered him as best she could. "I thought you might need this," she whispered, concerned. "The floor gets awful cold at night."

Big John propped himself on one elbow and his large features crinkled into a warm grin. "Thank you, Jennifer."

She smiled and gave him a hug.

Chapter 5

The bright shapes danced together briefly, moved away to mate with newer ones and then moved on still. Lying on her back Rose Marie could do nothing but watch the ceiling with its strange, candle-inspired shapes. Black silken cords held her immobile, a sour tasting gag was in her mouth, and she wore a long white gown, which she had no recollection of ever seeing, much less putting on. She was aware only of the throbbing pain in her lower jaw, the hardness of the bench on which she lay, and the dancing golden-gray shapes above her.

Rose Marie heard a door open, and Matthew Hudson peered down at her.

"I see my captive has awakened. That's good. It's getting late and I wouldn't want you to miss any of the festivities I have planned for this evening."

Matthew spoke cheerily as he leered at her. "It wouldn't do for the guest-of-honor to sleep through her greatest performance," he said, nodding respectfully. "When you told me you'd let me have your daughters, I believed you. Stupid me! I should have realized a mother's love for her children was too powerful to overcome."

She could smell his pungent body odor and his rotten breath whenever he came near. He stunk of sweat and decay.

Matthew saw the fear in her eyes as he came closer. "Please don't be afraid. I am going to make you more comfortable."

Rose Marie struggled against her bonds.

Matthew raised the end of the bench so her feet touched the floor. Rose Marie stood six feet from a stone hearth with a small fire.

"Do you like fireplaces, my dear?" Matthew asked matter-of-factly, almost casually. He might have been chatting about the weather.

Because of the gag, Rose Marie could only stare at him hatefully.

"I love them. You should, too," Matthew said as he bent to pick up a poker and tend the fire. "It may be the last thing you'll ever see."

Matthew paused and looked up at her. "You'll notice I said, 'may be'. If you give me your children, I'll let you live. If not, you must die. Quite simple really. Your life . . . or theirs."

Rose Marie struggled trying to shout through the gag, but she could only manage a muffled response.

"No need to answer now." Matthew held up a very large and very yellow hand. "Take your time. Think about it. Meanwhile, I'll prepare the props for your next performance." Matthew set down the poker and left the room.

Rose Marie was alone with her thoughts and what should have been a warm fire, but was not. The flames were strangely cold, like everything else in this weird, fantasy room.

True, I had agreed to sell my children, but I only wanted to make things better for them, Rose Marie thought. *Ivor and I could never provide the opportunities that a rich family could.* Rose Marie knew her actions were still wrong, but Matthew had promised her he would not harm them and he had lied. Rose Marie did not know what made her think she could go through with such a fiendish bargain. *I'd never turn them over to him. Never! No matter what he might do to me!*

Matthew returned carrying a metal box in one hand and a seven-foot copper tube in the other. The box was two feet long and had a scarred iron-gray surface, but it was the tube that held Rose Marie's interest. She had never seen anything like it before. The tube was ten inches wide, closed at one end and slightly flared at the other. Matthew turned it upside down and two pairs of metal legs slid out.

He attached the legs to clips on the underside of the tube and spread them to form an inverted double V.

Matthew set the waist-high tube before her. He placed the closed end over the fire and the flared front so tightly against her stomach that Rose Marie swore she could feel it scraping her spine every time she took a breath.

"This is a little invention of mine," Matthew announced, beaming proudly. "I like to call it the Hudson Rat Tube. In here," he patted the box, "I have three large rats. Fat, healthy rats which I have raised on the leavings of a meat-cutter's shop. They've become so used to flesh that they actually prefer it to their natural food. I haven't fed them in over a week, so I suspect they'll be quite hungry."

Matthew looked into her eyes to savor the fright he found there.

"If you choose not to help me, I'll put the rats into the tube. At one end the fire will make it unbearably hot while at the other your stomach will be blocking any chance for them to escape. I don't believe they'll spend much time trying to gnaw through the metal when you are so much more inviting."

Matthew moved closer, removing the gag from her mouth.

"Shall I put the rats into the tube?" he asked, his mouth salivating. "Or will you give me your children?"

"You might as well kill me because I'll never let you have them!" Her smile was brazen, full of contempt. She needed to hurt him badly, like he was doing to her. "I think you're enjoying this. Having a woman helpless. Is that the way you get your pleasure?" Rose Marie could tell by Matthew's tortured face that she had found a sore spot.

"You're pitiful! No woman would want you. Is this the only way you can get someone to pay attention? Maybe it's the only way you can get it up. Does the big man have to tie a woman up and watch her squirm to get his pleasure?"

Matthew managed a chuckle, but it sounded sick, not like laughter at all. "It makes no difference what you think of me. It doesn't hurt. Your decision not to help does, though. Perhaps my little friends will be more convincing than I."

Matthew reached into the burlap sack near his feet and took out some fatty scraps. He mashed them cruelly into her face and then stood back like an artist admiring his work. The grease highlighted Rose Marie's face. She spat a globule of fat from her lips.

Matthew wiped his hands on a cloth and carefully opened the box a crack. His hand shot inside and withdrew a gray squirming creature with a naked, pink tail. Matthew held the rat inches from

Rose Marie's face. She screeched in terror and thrust her face away from the pointed snout with its long chisel teeth. Matthew grabbed Rose Marie by the hair and jerked her head forward. She glanced in terror at the animal's black jewel eyes. Its nose was in constant motion, testing the air.

"Rats," Matthew explained, smiling at the small furry creature, its naked feet trying to scale an invisible ladder, "are called the lap dogs of the devil, and rightly so, for they do much of the Great One's bidding."

Matthew's smile was chilling as he brought the rat close enough to touch her ear.

A stabbing pain shot through Rose Marie's ear as the rat gnawed the fleshy appendage, and she let out a horrendous scream.

Matthew replaced the gag to keep her quiet, then watched engrossed as the animal greedily lapped the blood as it appeared. "Have you changed your mind?"

Rose Marie jerked her head from side to side, tears glistening on her cheeks.

"Very well," Matthew said, seizing her by the hair and thrusting her face within inches of the rodent. "Perhaps my lady wishes to see."

Matthew shoved the rat's crimson snout near Rose Marie's left nostril.

She felt him start to gnaw immediately and tried to erase the pain by thinking of something else. She thought about the time Ivor had taken the family on a picnic to the beach. It was a pleasant memory of a pleasant time and she needed such thoughts desperately right now. Rose Marie remembered, *She had boiled some pork the day before and made some sandwiches from freshly baked bread. Ivor had eaten two of them. She was so jealous because he'd always eat more than she and never gain an ounce.*

Matthew grunted in disgust and tried to jerk the rat away from the half-eaten nose. The animal refused to let go and clung to the cartilage with his teeth. He pulled harder and the creature came away with a piece of the rubbery, soft tissue. Matthew opened a door on top of the copper tube and placed the rat with the others.

Rose Marie remembered, *Ivor had found a pleasant shaded spot by the sea. He knew how she liked the water. It was so pretty and blue. She remembered she had never seen it more beautiful. Ivor had taken the girls for a walk while she had spread a blanket and sat enjoying the cool breeze, waiting for them to return. Soon she saw the girls racing back, their curls flying, Ivor slowing in the end to let Amy win. He eased to a walk holding Jennifer's hand: she was only five at the time. He joined her in the shade.*

Needle sharp teeth tore into Rose Marie's abdomen with savage fury.

The girls explored the beach while Ivor and she took a stroll. They listened to the gulls and watched the waves crash on the shore. He held her hand and told her he loved her like he used to, before they were married. He also told her how beautiful she was and how he couldn't live without her. She cried.

One of the sharp-toothed devils tunneled into her stomach with frenzied slashing.

When they had gotten back, she saw Amy had cornered a crab and was playfully prodding it with a stick, while Jennifer had collected over a dozen brightly colored shells and placed them on the blanket.

Rose Marie's insides were on fire with sharp slashing teeth and industrious clawing feet.

A—Amy had dropped her stick, Rose Marie struggled to concentrate, *to—to help . . . her sister. . . .*

All three rats had half their blood-blackened, furry bodies inside her. They were clawing, biting deeper.

Exasperated, Matthew took out his pocket watch and glanced at it. The mother had been of no help, and he was wasting too much time. Now he would have to handle matters in his own way, the way they should have been done in the first place.

Rose Marie's eyes fell on the glittering timepiece in Matthew's hand. The way the light shown on its surface seemed to attract her attention. She felt as though the watch was drawing her into it. That she was becoming one with it. As the life mercifully left her body, the gold watch was the last thing she saw.

Matthew saw her head loll forward and her body slump lifelessly against its bonds. He thrust the watch into his pocket and limped to the satanic chamber. Of the three doors in the building, this one was by far the heaviest. It was constructed of three-inch oak, sheathed in quarter-inch copper and had four broad hinges. The glow from thirteen candles on top of the altar flickered as the door opened.

They glinted on the beaten copper face of the door and it appeared to burn.

Matthew rolled back the oriental carpet, picked up the crimson pillow and brought it to the center of the magic circle. Now he went to the secret stone, pulled it out, and removed the cloth-shrouded knife, the scrap from the dress, and the lock of hair. He carried them to the pillow and knelt. Matthew took the black cloth from the ceremonial dagger and lovingly kissed the blade. He next jabbed the dagger into a crevice in the stone floor and rocked it deeper so it could stand by itself. Matthew took some straw from his pocket and wrapped it in the scrap of Jennifer's dress, then tied it with some twine. Finally, he took Jennifer's blonde hair, placed it on one end and tied it also. The pile of straw resembled a crude doll of the young girl. He tied the doll to the silver dagger with the goat's head handle towering over it.

Matthew closed his eyes and began to hum, his body swaying. As his swaying increased, so did the hum. Slowly he raised his head and broke into a chant. He was summoning the Great One to help capture the girl. His singing was vibrant and the room appeared to fluctuate with the movement of his body. Even the light from the candles waxed and waned in perfect rhythm. He was sweating heavily; the beads were oily and reflected the light. With his eyes closed and while his body swayed with the music, his hands searched for and found the black cloth and twine. His chanting became increasingly frantic, his movements more exaggerated. He placed the cloth over the doll and bound it with the twine. His singing reached a fever pitch, sweat ran down Matthew in rivulets, and the flames from the candles were leaping madly. The copper door became a confused swirling mass. It turned a brilliant shade of scarlet. Matthew kept his eyes shut. When he raised his arms, the immense sleeves of the robe fell back revealing thick-corded arms. Frothy spittle flew from his lips as his song got wilder. A small black speck appeared in the door, swelled and pulsed with the rhythm. Its black edges spread and attacked the flame of copper as its whip-like tentacles undulated, then joined to form a picture. First, it was a spider, then a vicious, snarling dog, its body black and muscular, its eyes blood-red. The edges wavered again and it was no longer a dog but a man. As the image became clearer, it appeared to be half-man, half-animal. The goat-like creature sat on a throne. His head and legs were covered with thick, shaggy hair and his feet were cloven hoofs. The arms and torso were human and naked and his eyes glowed molten red. Long curving horns grew from his head and about him flew bizarre, gargoylish creatures. Their gray skin was leathery and scaled and the wings were bat-like. Black forked tongues slithered from their mouths as they hovered, angling their reptilian heads this way and that.

The black cloth over the doll erupted into blue-white flames. Matthew swayed faster and wilder until he couldn't control himself any longer and pitched to the floor. He lay still, drained of energy. The candles slowly returned to their steady glow, and the door became reddish-brown copper again.

Chapter 6

Dawn didn't come fast enough for Ivor Noel Adamson. It crept ever so slowly, first lighting the horizon in a small faraway corner of the world, then blossoming like a great golden flower.

Ivor was up before the others, planning a strategy to rescue his wife. He, the constable, Bjorn Landstrom, and Amy would go to where his wife was being held captive and free her. Ivor didn't want to take any of the girls, but he needed someone to identify the man they were after. He had chosen Amy because she was older and had a greater eye for detail than her sister had. That ability might prove important. Big John would stay and watch Jennifer until their return.

It was seven o'clock by the time everyone was up and pushing eight-thirty before they ate, went over the plan, and set it into motion.

Jennifer quietly watched her father and the others leave. Her father and Mr. Landstrom waved—Amy stuck out her tongue.

Big John joined her in the doorway and placed his hands upon her shoulders. "Don't worry, Jennifer. They'll find your Mama."

Jennifer didn't look at him. She was too busy watching the others go. "I know they will." She moved to the hearth and saw the dying fire leftover from breakfast. She stoked it with more wood. She hated to see anything die right now.

Wanting to break the awkward silence, Big John asked, "Is there any more tea?"

Jennifer shook her head. "No, but I'll make some more." She was imitating her mother and acting grownup. The girl walked to the two oaken buckets and raised their lids. There wasn't enough water between them to float a good-sized walnut. "We need some water."

Big John crossed the floor in three even strides, picked up the buckets with one hand and held out the other for Jennifer. "Let's fetch some."

Jennifer took the huge hand and her face glowed. She suddenly felt very important because here was someone who wanted to be with her.

When John and Jennifer got to the well near the old church, they had to wait their turn. A tow-headed boy of eleven or twelve and an old woman with a black shawl were ahead of them. The boy filled his two buckets and left, but the woman was having trouble. She lowered her small pail easily enough, but was having difficulty raising it. Big John stepped forward to help her, took the rope, and pulled it up with no trouble. Like yesterday, he wore no shirt, and Jennifer watched with awe as his big arms worked.

After they had gotten water and were headed back, Big John observed that the morning was unusually calm. The night before had seen one of those tropical rarities that sometime occur. A blessed chilling breeze had swept in from the north bringing rain to the part of the island that needed it most. The rain had cooled Port Royal from the day's heat, but it had grown hot and sultry in a short time. Shimmering heat waves danced along the crowded waterfront buildings and quays that lined King's Street, while the merchants and their customers seemed more subdued and lethargic than usual. Even the sea was a flat, blue-green mirror, and the half dozen ships in the harbor rode slackly at their cables. There wasn't a breath of wind, or even a single bird on the wing to create the slightest breeze.

When Big John and Jennifer returned to the house, he went in first. From out of the shadows a screaming, iron poker slammed into his head and sent him crashing to the floor. Jennifer rushed inside to help, but when she did, Matthew Hudson stepped into the light and slammed the door.

*   *   *

Ivor and Bjorn knelt beside the body of Victor Chapman. His head, wig comically askew, had turned a swarthy purple from the heat. They were in the back room of the constable's office with the door ajar. Amy was peeking through the crack.

"I'd say the man's got a broken neck," Landstrom volunteered, straightening up and taking a pull on his pipe. He drew no smoke and took a silver pick from his pocket to loosen the ashes. His eyes followed Ivor's hand as it pulled the auburn wig aside, revealing the other half of the puffy face. The dead man's cheeks were so bloated from the heat that his eyes were mere slits. His mouth hung open and a fly buzzed out, flew in a tight circle, and landed on the cracked lips.

"I wonder what happened?" Ivor asked with a puzzled tone in his voice.

Bjorn shrugged and looked around. "I don't know, but I'll wager he didn't slip on those." He motioned to the dusty floor with its scattering of banana peels.

Ivor nodded.

Amy pushed the door wider. She was all eyes to take in her surroundings better. "The man who kidnapped us did it."

Ivor forgot about ordering her not to come in and eyed her curiously. "You saw him kill the constable?"

"No, but I did see him with Mr. Chapman right after Jennifer and I escaped."

Both men were listening. Bjorn stopped fussing with his pipe.

"The big, scary man was arguing with the constable. That's when Jennifer and I left to find you," Amy's voice grew weak with self-doubt, not knowing if she had done the right thing. After all, a man had died.

Ivor put a hand on his daughter's shoulder. "You did exactly what you should have. Nothing could have been done. Even if you tried to help, he might have killed you, too."

Amy smiled, pleased.

"Can you find the man's house from here?" Ivor asked.

"Yes, but it may be the same place that I took you to yesterday."

That's all right. Maybe things will appear differently in the daylight."

Ivor took his daughter's hand, and the three of them walked to the meat-cutter's shop.

*   *   *

Jennifer backed away from the demon before her.

Wearing an insane grin, Matthew Hudson moved forward with deliberate slowness. He relished the girl's helplessness and did not want to rush the thrill of his latest triumph.

Jennifer moved so the table was between them. The big man swept it aside easily, never taking his eyes from her. The girl wanted to run, but she knew she was not fast enough. Jennifer backed along the wall and nearly tripped on something. A quick glance revealed the doll her Papa had made for her.

Matthew was closer.

The youngster snatched the doll off the floor. It wasn't a weapon, but it was the only thing she had. It had a cloth body, but its head was hard baked clay. She sidled to her left—closer to the door.

Matthew was nearer, his dark shadow looming over her.

She needed to get a head start, just a second or so.

Jennifer pretended to clutch the doll helplessly to her chest while tensing every muscle. When Matthew was nearly upon her, she hurled it at him.

The doll slammed into his left eye with a blinding flash.

Jennifer heard him howl in rage. She bolted to her right and the distance to the door seemed farther than ever. Everything she did seemed to be in slow-motion.

She was building speed—getting closer to the door.

Two more strides.

Steely fingers bit into her left shoulder from behind.

She was still going.

A ripping sound filled the air as the material of her dress gave way.

Another loping stride. A second crushing hand was hauling her back.

Jennifer clawed for the door, but couldn't reach it. An obscene chortle came to her from behind and chilled her to the bone.

Suddenly the hands were gone.

Jennifer made the door, glanced back and saw Big John with his arms around Matthew.

The men grappled, and then broke apart. Big John's head was a sheet of blood as he crouched with arms spread. "So, the big, tough man who likes to kidnap little girls is back. Let's see how tough you are against a grown man."

Matthew imitated the other man perfectly, the crouch, the open arms, even the blatant look of hate.

The men circled each other, trying to gain an advantage.

Jennifer stayed behind Big John.

The men continued to circle. Big John made an explosive rush; his fist sent Matthew reeling into the table. From outward appearances the blow seemed to have little effect, but the spreading red stain on his lower lip told a different story. He shoved Big John away and dragged his hand across his mouth. "You'll pay for that," Matthew promised. As he spoke, blood trickled down his beard and onto the black shirt.

They did not bother circling this time, but rushed straight ahead and met with a brutal thunderclap, flailing away with massive, club-like fists. This time Matthew got the better exchange.

When they separated, Big John wore a fresh coat of blood. He was so evenly covered that it was impossible to tell from which of the half dozen wounds the new blood sprang.

In the space of a heartbeat, they locked in combat again. Big John shoved Matthew up against the wall and hammered at the other man's face.

It was very slight at first, a barely audible rumbling deep within the earth. Jennifer heard it. The men might have too, if they had not been so busy trying to tear each other apart. The building shook as if it were alive; windows rattled and some grains of sand and plaster rained down. Jennifer ran outside. Terrified screams filled the air as dozens of people rushed into the street, some dropping to their knees and praying, others wringing their hands and crying. Even the dust on the ground shook so it made its own low hanging cloud.

An explosive crack in the earth shot between the two men and threw them apart. Big John leaped clear. Matthew lost his balance and fell into the crack, plummeting to his shoulders. Only the tremendous strength of his arms kept him from falling farther. The slight motion of retrieving his watch from a shirt pocket made him slip farther. Matthew did not even notice his fingers becoming torn and bloody while trying to halt the slide. He was too busy staring childlike at the engraving of the ship on the timepiece's cover. In the swirling dust and half-light of hell the case seemed to glow alive. Matthew squeezed his eyes tight and wished himself small, so small he could slip into the ship and sail out of the yawning crack. Another tremor caused his body to slide into the crack farther.

No! he thought, *Not yet! I can't fall yet!*

Matthew concentrated with his whole mind and being. McDowell's voice came to him and said, *"It caught a wee bit'o magic when it was made, Laddie. If'n ya truly believe, it'll take yer soul and sail forever."*

Matthew felt his grip weaken and flung the watch as far as he could. It tumbled end-over-end while Matthew fell to his doom.

Big John staggered out the door and into the street. He heard a deafening whoosh and saw a tremendous wall of water behind Jennifer. The wave was muddy gray, towering some fifty feet and swallowing everything in its path. Big John raced to the girl, shielding her with his body as the wave crashed over them.

Even though John had no control over where the rushing water was carrying him, he was still able to maintain a tight grip on Jennifer. Big John swam the best he could, knowing that soon the water would recede and become calm enough for them to make shore.

*   *   *

When the earthquake began Amy and Ivor didn't know what was happening. Ivor had seen Bjorn swallowed by a monstrous crack that had raced across the street, then watched in horror as it closed again. The earth seemed to chew the struggling man until his insides shot from his mouth, then the crack opened again swallowing him whole. Ivor grabbed Amy and ran so fast he nearly outran the wall of water that crashed down on them. The wave killed Ivor instantly, but it swept Amy along and deposited alive in a tree.

Big John became the perfect father for the girls because now he had the family he had always dreamed of.

*   *   *

Despite the disaster, Port Royal remained undaunted. It returned to its wicked ways by nightfall, and thieves robbed the bodies as they washed ashore. Some people felt that remaining on land wasn't safe and sought refuge elsewhere. The few ships that survived the tidal wave were only too glad to accommodate them, and their crews charged the frightened people exorbitant sums to be allowed a precious berth on their crowded decks.

Though the rebuilding of Port Royal began at once, it never regained its reputation as "The Wickedest City on Earth."

Chapter 7

THE EXCAVATION

Friday, July 3, 2010, Port Royal, Jamaica

Mike Ryan was in twenty-five feet of water watching the hypnotic clouds of silt take on new streamlined shapes as they sped up and elongated in the current. That current was created by the hungry mouth of the five-inch water dredge, which like a terrible monster, swallowed not only the wispy clouds but also anything else in its path.

Mike and his partner, Paul Kushe, were working at the bottom of Kingston Harbor doing a feasibility study for the Jamaican National Trust. Their job was to look for artifacts from the sunken city of Port Royal so it could be determined what to do with the harbor. The government wanted to expand the deep-water port close to Kingston to accommodate more cruise ships and commercial freighters with their deep drafts. Cruises had become popular with today's tourists, and the Jamaican economy didn't want a single ship to be turned away by something as trivial as their shallow southwestern harbor.

Port Royal was ideally suited for the proposed dredging because of its natural harbor and its proximity to Jamaica's largest city, Kingston. Like most good things, however, this one was saddled with a curse. That curse was the sunken city of Port Royal. Before the government could begin dredging the project needed to be cleared with the Jamaican National Trust. The Trust oversees the cultural treasures of the island and since Port Royal sank into the sea from a violent earthquake on June 7, 1692, they considered it a national treasure. What the Trust needed to know was this: Does anything substantial exist after all these years, and if it does should they excavate it? They brought in Mike Ryan and his team of divers to answer those questions.

About five months before, Mr. Wilkens, director of the Jamaican National Trust, had explained that the government had allocated a small percentage of their 2010 budget to the Trust.

Due to the limited funds and equipment available to him, Mike settled on six people who could perform several jobs well. The six people were all divers, and their areas of expertise were:

1. Mike Ryan, underwater archaeologist and head of the project

2. Mark Sullivan, photographer

3. Paul Kushe, carpenter

4. Tom Marino, mechanic

5. Nick Hynes, welder

6. Barbara Anderson, underwater archaeologist in charge of artifact cleaning and preservation

The Jamaican National Trust added John Reid, a government employee. His qualifications were electrician, diver and amateur underwater archaeologist.

*　　*　　*

Paul Kushe knifed his fingers into the chalky sand and pushed toward the center of the dredge's widening hole. Fingers were the primary digging tools because they were sensitive and would not hurt anything delicate. He created the billowy clouds that drifted upon the current until the bucking dredge swallowed them. The two men were excavating the remains of a wall. Paul would remove a little sand from one side, then swim over the wall and remove the same amount on the other. This evened the pressure on each side and guarded against collapse.

Mike held onto the vibrating nozzle for all he was worth although his strength, like the sand, was quickly vanishing. He renewed his grip on the brass handle, but found he had lost the feeling in his fingers. Mike was feeling the vibrations to his very core when mercifully the vacuum-like machine bucked once, then lay still. Someone had turned off the water pump, or else it had run out of fuel. Either way, he welcomed the break and gave Paul the thumbs-up to head for the surface and lunch.

Mike left the nozzle on the bottom to mark the spot where they were working, then swam up to the shadow of the bobbing inflatable boat. Grabbing the Zodiac's side, he tossed his mask and fins into the boat before pulling himself aboard. Paul had stripped off his gear and had begun hauling up the yellow basket containing the morning's finds. When it came aboard Paul picked up two oyster-colored chunks of conglomerate and began tapping them together. He resembled a caveman trying to fashion a tool or start a fire. The pieces clicked at a furious pace until a large portion broke away.

"Don't do that, Paul," Mike snapped in irritation. He was tired and drained from his shift with the one-eyed monster, the pet name the dredge had acquired. "Barbara would have your hide if she knew what you were doing."

Paul frowned but did not answer. He was examining the piece with interest. Mike gathered up their dive gear and set it aside, then turned to the Johnson outboard and primed it. The warmth of the sun felt so good Mike closed his eyes for a minute.

"Hey! Look at this!" Paul moved forward holding something small and golden in a white, wrinkled hand. The small boat shared his enthusiasm and rocked with excitement. "I think it's a gold watch or something."

Paul sat down on the air chamber on Mike's side of the boat and was used a stubby thumbnail to remove some stubborn incrustation.

"Here, let me see." The request sounded more like an order than Mike had intended.

Paul placed the trinket in the other man's hand.

Mike had seen many calcified lumps reveal just a black powder oxide when they were broken open, a mere shadow of the rusted iron that had once been. However this was different; it was gold, about the size of a silver dollar, but thicker, and the case was engraved with a beautiful three-masted ship. Mike's fingers moved to a latch on the side and to his amazement the case popped open. "Unbelievable," was all he could manage.

Paul jockeyed for position. "Let me see!"

Silver sulfide blackened the pocket watch's face, but it was possible to make out the faint roman numerals representing the hours. The hands had rusted away. Left in their place were two thin reddish-brown stains that showed the exact time the watch had registered before its submersion—probably the exact time of the disaster. A name was engraved inside the front cover—Matthew Hudson. Mike suddenly felt uncomfortable and handed the watch to Paul. "Here. Let's go," Mike snapped, looking and sounding very much like the impatient boss that he tried hard not to be.

"What's the hurry?"

Mike gazed at the cloudless sky and shrugged his shoulders. "I just want to get back. Okay?"

Mike turned the key and started the motor. Realizing that it was time to go, Paul put down the watch and untied the inflatable from its mooring buoy. Mike took the tiller, opened the throttle all the way and aimed the boat for the shore. It was a short ride, barely five hundred feet, but in that time Mike turned to look at the watch at least twice. Each time he peered at it he could not shake the feeling of something being terribly wrong.

The group of six men and one woman sat around the long picnic table eating fried grouper with beans and wild rice and swapped stories of the morning's activities. Their dining room was an open-air porch with poles spaced ten feet apart to support the thatched roof. The crude structure appeared rustic and quaint, but it was really a marvel of engineering. It was the equivalent of air-conditioning without any moving parts or outrageous electric bills, while the roof shaded the interior, and the absence of walls let the cooling sea breezes through. Nature's own was working to full capacity for a pleasant breeze came off the water and swept past the relaxing group.

"So, Mike, tell me about the watch," Barbara asked as she examined the case. Her calm demeanor spoke of professional curiosity, but her blue eyes glinted with excitement.

"Well, Paul found it buried in sand and wedged between some rocks in a wall." Mike tried to appear casual, but wanted to prolong his conversation with the only woman on the outing. "Being buried helped to preserve it. Do you think it'll clean up okay?"

"Yes, I believe it will. I'll get on it after lunch."

Barbara had become a fine archaeologist, thought Mike, and he was lucky to get her for this job. He had known her at Texas A&M when she began her studies there. He also knew that she had been one of those girls, a typical golden girl, who throughout high school and college was undoubtedly captain of the cheerleaders and the prettiest girl in school.

Barbara's face brightened when she found the latch and the case popped open. "Oh Mike. Isn't this gorgeous!"

"It sure is," Mike agreed. He was looking at Barbara and not the watch.

She became puzzled. "There's an inscription inside. Matthew. . . . "

"Matthew Hudsen," he helped.

"I wonder who he was?" Barbara said, looking up. "I would say a nobleman at least, judging by the quality and workmanship I see here."

"No, he wasn't," Paul said as he speared another piece of grouper on his plate. "He was probably a pirate."

Both she and Mike looked toward him. He set his fork down and slid closer to Barbara on the bench.

"Uh—uh. He was a man of obvious taste and means. Look at the elegance of this case," she said, holding it up for inspection. "Does this look like something a thief would own?"

"That doesn't mean a thing. Port Royal was full of pirates. Look at your history."

She turned to Mike for support. "Mike, what do you think?" A shining strand of baby fine hair dipped below one eye. She brushed it back. The wind immediately flipped it into her face again.

"Well," Mike began, trying to sound scholarly, "you're both right. It probably did belong to someone of wealth and position, but it may have been pirate booty also. We need to know more at this point. We'll try to trace the owner and find out who Matthew Hudsen was."

Barbara turned to Paul trying to figure out if she had won a victory. Deciding she had, she spat out triumphantly, "See! I told you I was right."

Paul smiled. "I didn't say a pirate had it made. I only said it belonged to one. The only taste those thieves had was in their mouths."

Barbara laughed and Paul joined her, gradually shifting Mike out of the conversation. The two of them bantered back and forth. A few self-conscious minutes later, Mike got up, grabbed his autographed copy of Sidney Sheldon's *MASTER OF THE GAME*, and walked into the harsh Jamaican sun.

He spread a towel on the gray sand and lay down, making himself as comfortable as he could on his stomach, and opened the book. The warming radiance of the sun felt good on his back, and the breeze ruffled his thick, black hair. Mike's eyes were a warm sea-green and the sun pleasantly weathered his thirty-six-year-old face. After reading for several minutes, he closed the book and set it down on the towel. He was too distracted to read. His thoughts kept returning to his conversation at lunch.

Damn Paul! Damn Paul and Barbara both! Mike was jealous. He didn't want to be, but he was. He guessed he felt the way he did because the other man possessed everything he did not. Paul was rich and ruggedly handsome, a typical ex-jock, while Mike struggled to make a living and considered himself only above average in looks. Paul didn't need this job in the monetary sense; he had all the money he could ever want. His father's wealth from construction saw to that. The more that Mike thought about the two of them together, the madder he got, so he chose not to think about them at all. Instead, he thought about his other passion, diving.

Ever since Mike was little he had wanted to dive beneath the waves and learn the mysteries of the sea. Before he was old enough to take formal scuba lessons, he collected all the books he could about the underwater world and read them from cover to cover at least twice. One reading was for the story; the second reading was for the parts he liked best. These stories were usually about shipwrecks or treasure.

The day after Mike turned fifteen, he signed up for scuba lessons at the YMCA. When it came time to make his first plunge he did so easily. With scuba, he was free! He was free to swim with the fish and to learn their secrets, free to explore and create his own adventures.

As Mike grew older, he expanded his love for water and directed his interest toward underwater archaeology, shipwrecks in particular. He enrolled in the Underwater Archaeology Program at Texas A&M University where he had graduated with honors. Since then his life had been complete . . . or so he thought.

Barbara popped into Mike's mind. He saw her vividly. She was looking out to sea—her hair loose and flowing. Suddenly she was not alone anymore. Paul was there, holding her, loving her.

Mike tried to forget her and thought about diving again. It wasn't easy because she kept fading in and out. He would think about the water, and then she would be there, naked, as if she had just gone for a midnight swim—her hair and face wet, sexy. She would move forward to kiss him with moist, parted lips. Then she'd grow pale and disappear. Suddenly Paul was there grinning.

Mike thought about diving again. *Funny how your body can get so cold . . .*

She reappeared vaguely, her color pale, indistinct around the edges.

Mike shook his head, forcing the thought of her from his mind. He began again, *Funny how your body can get so cold from being in such warm water. It was eighty-seven degrees and—*

She appeared again—paler this time.

Mike tuned her out and continued with the unfinished thought. *Warm water being cold? Must have something to do with water being denser than air—carrying away the body heat faster.* He considered this and yawned. Diving always made him sleepy.

Mike saw her again, in the water. This time he didn't wait for her to come to him. He moved forward, a strange gliding walk. They met and kissed passionately. The kiss (the sun?) felt warm and intoxicating. A smile creased Mike's lips, and he began to doze.

Paul held the pocket watch and glanced after Barbara as she left the table. *Christ, she was beautiful—an absolute goddess.* Her lithe form with its golden tan, white Bermuda shorts and matching halter-top presented a striking figure. At twenty-seven Barbara had silken hair of spun gold that curled naturally about her delicate shoulders. She moved with the regal grace and elegance Paul admired in a woman. It seemed Barbara brought a touch of class to everything she did, and the most mundane chores suddenly seemed marvelous and exciting.

With Barbara gone from view, Paul turned his attention to the watch and thumbed the case. It opened easily and he marveled at its magnificent preservation and workmanship. "Well, Mr. Matthew Hudsen, where you are you won't need this watch anymore."

Paul suddenly grimaced in pain and dropped the watch as if it had been red hot. His headache was so intense that he wanted to cry out, but his macho image would not let him. Just when he thought he could stand the pain no longer, it stopped as quickly as it had started. Relieved that it was over, Paul sneaked a look at the others to see if he was being observed. He was sure he hadn't been because Mark Sullivan had everyone's attention and was acting his usual offbeat self. He had placed a stainless steel bowl on his head, was holding a long tapered cigar, and was speaking in a high nasal voice while the others guffawed and tossed in their barbs.

Paul got up and took a few steps when he realized he had forgotten the watch. The moment that he retrieved it, he rubbed his forehead. The headache had begun again. Paul set the pocket watch on the workbench in the dive shack and went back outside, massaging his throbbing temples with both hands.

"What's the matter, mister? Your head hurt?"

Paul looked up to find a young barefoot girl of about six or seven. She had a cute little nose and large brown eyes that could melt any man's heart.

"Yes, it does."

"Maybe it's from being in the water too long."

"It could be," he agreed, then asked, "What's your name?"

"Kristen. What's yours?"

"Mine's Paul. You live around here?"

"Uh—huh, right over there," she said, pointing to the brightly painted houses beyond the encampment.

"What kind of things do you do in the water, Paul?"

"I look for all sorts of things."

"Like what?"

The inquisitive little girl with the big brown eyes and the long, delicate lashes captivated Paul. "I find old things that have become lost."

"Why?"

"Because it's my job."

"Oh. I lost a toy boat over there. Would you find it for me?"

"Sure. What does it look like?"

She held her hands about six inches apart. "Well, it was about that long and red."

Paul walked over to the spot she had pointed to. "Over here?"

She nodded and moved to the water's edge. "I put Molly on it, and it sank."

"Who's Molly?"

"My dolly. She can't swim."

Paul had to smile. "Are you sure? I'll bet we'll find her, and she'll be good as new."

"Bet we won't."

"Oh, but I'm good at finding things. Remember?"

She nodded enthusiastically.

"What's that?" Paul asked, cupping his hand to his ear.

The little girl faced the water and placed both hands behind her ears, listening intently.

"Do you hear that?"

She shook her head no.

"Maybe you're not close enough." Paul picked Kristen up and walked to the water. "Come on, we'll find Molly. I think I heard her calling your name."

Kristen burst into tears. "Stop! Let me down!"

"What's wrong?"

"I'm afraid! I can't swim, and my mommy won't let me go near the water. She said bad things can happen!"

Paul set her on the sand. "What did she tell you?"

"She said there's a monster that lives under the water, and he eats little children."

"There's no monster out there, Kristen. I've been underwater, and I know."

She stared up at him with childlike wonder. "There's not?"

"Heck no. If you'll come with me I'll help you find your boat and your dolly."

"You will!"

"Yes, ma'am, I promise!"

She looked around to make sure her mother was not watching. "Okay!" She climbed into his arms, and they waded into the water.

Paul shaded his eyes with his free hand and walked around in the shallow water. Finally, he saw something red beneath the surface, and he reached down and brought out the boat.

Kristen squealed with joy and reached for her toy. She examined it, and replied, "But Molly's not here? Where's Molly?"

"Just a minute. I hear something." Paul felt around in the water again. He raised her lost, dripping wet doll. "Here she is! I heard her call your name."

"You did?"

"Uh—huh."

Kristen hugged his neck and kissed his cheek. "I love you, Paul! You saved Molly!"

"Wow! You're easy to please," Paul said, as he walked back to shore. The little girl's charm worked like magic, his headache had disappeared.

"Kristen?" A woman's voice called from the direction of the houses.

The girl looked at Paul sadly, clutching her doll and her red boat. "That's my mommy. She's looking for me, so I guess I'd better go."

He nodded. "That's probably a good idea. It was a pleasure meeting you, Kristen."

"Bye, Paul," She said, then scampered away to the woman who had just appeared near the diver's living quarters.

Chapter 8

⚓

Captain Anthony took a red handkerchief from his back pocket, removed his battered straw hat and mopped his brow while deciding his best course of action. The old black man's blue gingham shirt was sweat-stained and the faded material hung limp, but the fatiguing heat had not diluted his resolve a bit. He replaced the hat, pulled the brim low, and followed the dog into the mangroves.

The trees leafy canopy provided a pleasant sanctuary from the searing wrath of the sun, and all things that grew here profited from its shelter. Unlike the arid conditions outside, this was a small, rich world filled with life. An insect buzzed the man's ear as if telling him an incredible secret, and plants of every description grew in wild abundance. Captain Anthony brushed the pesky bug away while parting the leathery leaves.

Where had Prince gone? He must meet the young man soon.

Captain Anthony quickened his pace. He stumbled over a gnarled root raised five-inches above the ground and fell on his left arm; his frail shoulder absorbed the impact, making him wince. It seemed the older he became the more his body complained, and the more it complained the louder it got. Right now, his body was screaming. The old man sat on the ground massaging the nagging shoulder. A small, brown lizard scurried to the side of a tree and fixed the intruder with a level stare.

Captain Anthony needed a rest and sat looking at his surroundings. The branches of the canopy rustled in the wind, emitting twinkling sapphires of blue sky that illuminated the scrub brush, wild pine, and a choking undergrowth of various ferns and weeds. After a bit, Captain Anthony picked up the shabby straw hat, punched it into its former shape and placed it on his head. He struggled to his feet and began slowly walking. The dog had disappeared, and the need for haste was gone.

After five minutes, Captain Anthony's surroundings became brighter. He could see large patches of blue sky where none had existed before. The foliage grew sparser until it abruptly stopped at the beach. He saw the young man, his young man, lying on the sand. He was about to venture onto the beach when a girl approached.

Urgent splashing caught the old man's attention. He shaded his eyes and saw his dog running into the surf. The animal swam fifty or sixty yards, then cut in toward the shore and headed toward the couple.

The girl had joined the man, and they were talking. Prince yelped and they turned to look at the water. The dog was struggling to stay above the breakers, but every once in a while his head dipped beneath the crashing waves. The young man ran into waist deep water, picked up the limp animal and carried him to the sand. Sensing that all was well, Captain Anthony broke into a grin and left.

*   *   *

The beach was breathtaking. The delicate turquoise of the water melted into the silver-gray sand of the beach; the beach in turn blended into the wild tangles of mangroves and beyond them azure mountains capped the lush viridian vegetation in the distance. In those mountains, it rained almost every afternoon, spilling the life-giving water down their slopes and feeding coffee, banana, and sugar cane.

Barbara noticed the lone figure lying on the beach. She found herself drawn to Mike's location and soon was looking down at him. "Why did you go away?"

Mike squinted, trying to focus on her. The sun was bright, and he shielded his eyes. "I didn't."

"Of course you did."

"I didn't go away from you. I. . .ah . . . wanted to get some sun before we have to get back to work."

Barbara gazed at him and folded her arms. An awkward silence passed between them while both thought of what to say next.

"I really . . . ," he began.

"But, I didn't . . . ," she said.

They spoke at once and laughed.

"I'm sorry," Mike said. "You first."

Barbara nodded her appreciation and sat next to him. "What I wanted to say is that I hope you didn't leave on my account."

Mike became puzzled. "Why would I do that?"

She shrugged. "You know how men get. They sometimes act funny when there's another man around."

"Oh, that. I didn't mind."

"Well good. Then I don't feel so bad."

Barbara hugged her knees into her chest and wondered what she would have to do to get Mike to notice her. A dog's panicked barking caused Mike to turn away. Barbara swung around, her problem forgotten.

A dog bobbed in the surf several hundred feet away. The two scrambled to the water's edge and watched as the dog reached the breakers. The wave crested and fell, pushing him forward with a tremendous rush. The dog surfaced, whimpering; his head barely above water. Mike splashed into the surf, gathered him in his arms and brought him ashore. He looked half-dead, not able to hold his head up.

Mike set him down to examine him. His fur was light brown; he had a collar but no tags; and he looked like he could be a Labrador retriever. His muzzle raised above the sand a few inches, then quickly dropped back. The effort must have been too much because he was whimpering in pain.

"Oh, you poor thing!" Barbara moaned, melting to her knees to comfort him. She stroked the glossy head and neck, and asked, "What do you think happened?"

"I don't know," Mike answered, kneeling next to her. "Maybe he just strayed too far."

Barbara continued petting the dog. He raised his head to look at her, his amber eyes glowing. "Are you okay?"

Still shaking from his ordeal, the dog raised enough to rest on his haunches.

"Look at that!" she observed. "See how he immediately responds to a few kind words. I'll bet he's simply starved for affection."

The dog was nuzzling her hand and looking alert.

Mike stroked the dog's shoulders and back. "Say, fellow, do you want to come home with us?"

The dog turned to him and squeaked a tail-wagging reply.

Barbara could not believe her ears. Glaring at Mike she said, "Of course, he's coming with us! Were you just going to leave him here?"

She swiveled back to the dog with a flourish and cooed to him, "Don't listen to the mean man, pretty baby. You'll stay with me."

Swaying unsteadily, the lab got to his feet, and sat back down.

Barbara placed her hands on Mike's chest, her face pleading. "He can't stand. Would you carry him?"

"I don't know if we should take him away from the beach. His owner may be looking for him."

Barbara knelt to stroke his coat. "I'll keep an eye out for anyone. I just want to get him out of the sun and give him something to eat."

The man eyed the canine. "He doesn't look starved to me."

"Mike, please?"

"Oh, all right!" Mike gathered the dog into his arms and lifted him.

As the two of them walked toward the dining hall, Mike said, "You know we can't go on calling him Pretty Baby forever. He has to have a name."

"You're right," Barbara admitted. The wind tugged at her hair, flipped it into her face. She brushed it back and it promptly came forward again. She brightened. "How about Brownie?"

"You've got to be kidding."

"What's wrong with that?" she demanded. "I once had a dog named Brownie."

Mike didn't answer. He glanced at his burden. "I've got a better idea."

"Better than Brownie? I doubt it."

"I've got a name that really fits him. Since he's being carried like one, how about King?"

Barbara considered this. "I don't know. I still like Brownie." Her eyes sparkled and she laughed. "However, I think I like King better."

They began walking again, her petting and him carrying.

*   *   *

Mike aimed the twelve-foot inflatable at the two candy-cane striped inner-tubes floating within seven feet of each other. One supported the water pump for the dredge and the other held a small compressor that fed air to the divers through a "Hookah" system. Since the men were working in shallow water for extended periods there was no need to carry the short-lived and cumbersome diving tanks. Instead, they wore a large mask that covered the entire face, allowing them to breathe and talk normally. The system had one drawback, however: Wherever the diver went he was tethered to the compressor by one hundred feet of white air hose, thus limiting his range.

Mike throttled down the laboring outboard as they glided smoothly into the space between the inner tubes, nudging them gently. He killed the motor and asked, "How about taking the dredge this afternoon?"

"What?" Paul answered feebly, his face wan. "Oh, the dredge. Sure."

"Are you feeling okay?"

"I—I don't know. I felt fine all morning, but after lunch I got this lousy headache. Must have been something I ate."

Mike grew concerned. "You don't look so good. I'll go into shore and get somebody to replace you."

"No. I'll be all right when we get into the water. The headache isn't so bad, but I seem to be in a fog."

"That settles it! You're not diving today." Mike turned to start the motor.

"Mike, I'm okay to dive."

"No, you're not. You're a danger to yourself and to me. I don't want anyone hurt on this trip. It's not worth it," Mike said with total authority, ending the conversation.

Suddenly, Paul leaped across the boat and seized Mike by the throat. The flimsy inflatable sagged under their combined load and flipped the struggling men into the water.

Mike's world burst into white water and bubbles as the two thrashed about. The shock of the water made Paul release his grip. He appeared bewildered.

Mike cleared his throat with difficulty and glared at his opponent while trying to maintain a margin of safety between them.

"Keep away, Paul!" Mike warned, trying to sound threatening. He didn't recognize the low scratchy voice as his. "I don't want to hurt you!"

Paul looked around as if seeing the water for the first time and not knowing what to make of it.

"What happened? Do you need help?"

"No, I don't!" Mike snapped as he approached the other man cautiously. When the two were within touching distance, he blew up.

"What the hell was that all about?"

"I'm not sure. The last thing I remember is we were in the boat, and I guess you decided to take me back to shore."

Mike looked dubious. "You don't remember anything else? How do you think we got into the water?"

"I don't know."

Mike regarded him strangely. "Okay! Forget it, but I want you to get in the boat first."

Paul nodded and swam to the side of the inflatable. He pulled himself up and the boat down until they met halfway, and he slid aboard. He extended a hand to Mike.

Only the lapping of the waves against the boat broke the tense silence between them. After what seemed a long moment, Mike took the offered hand and climbed aboard the inflatable.

When they reached the shore, both men dragged the boat onto the beach. Paul dejectedly sat on the gray softness of the inflatable and watched Mike gather up his gear and head to the dive shack. He felt both bewilderment and regret. Bewilderment at what had happened and regret at having let his friend down. Mike was a true friend and had shown confidence in Paul when he was low and needed it most. Mike had given him a break letting him come to Jamaica and then by working with him personally. Paul knew Mike liked having him around, especially when there was work to be done. Paul worked very hard and rarely needed a break. As far back as Paul could remember he had always enjoyed pitching in and helping his father in the concrete business. He didn't mind the backbreaking labor, the dirt and sweat involved, and the long hours it sometimes demanded. It was his way of saying thank you. Thank you for putting your faith and trust in me.

Paul would make a game of his work when he grew as big as the other laborers. He would always try to be the best at everything. At first, Paul had always lost. However, he soon outgrew the others, not only in size, but in strength and skills as well. It got so none of the others wanted to work with Paul anymore. It became a form of punishment to work alongside him because no matter how hard the laborers would try, he'd always show them up, sometimes very badly. The men would laugh and call him a freak behind his back. Soon Paul was ostracized from the very group he wanted to impress. When he would turn to his father for help, he found he was alone, as always. Paul could not go to his mother. She had died when he was two years old.

Paul's father had a unique way of handling his son's problems. He was an avid cigar smoker who wielded the stubby, chewed end like a weapon. When Paul told him of his problem, which very rarely happened—usually his father didn't have time to listen, he'd take the stogy out of his mouth, smile a bit and say, "Don't worry, Son. You need friends? Here, this'll buy lots of 'em." He would pull a wad of bills from his pocket, peel off a few and give them to Paul. Mostly they'd be twenties or fifties and sometimes, depending upon the problem, Paul might find a couple of hundreds. "Girls, too," he would say, peeling off a few more bills and shoving them into his son's hand. "Girls cost more. They like to be shown a good time. Impresses the hell out of 'em." That was his father; money was the magic cure-all that solved everything. If you had it and flaunted it, you were in command. His father could never see that money was not the solution. Paul only wanted to be liked for himself.

Paul was sorry and afraid for having let his friend down. He was worried the blackout might reveal that he was sick and he could not work the excavation anymore.

It wasn't fair, Paul thought, *I only want to be accepted. That's all I ever wanted!*

"Hi, Paul."

Paul glanced up. The little girl he had met the other day was there holding a large purple flower.

"Hi, Kristen!"

"You look sad. Does your head hurt again?"

Paul gave Kristen a big smile to show her that he was indeed all right. "It did, but not anymore. You chased my headache away."

She giggled. "I did?"

"Yes! No headache stands a chance against that smile."

She grinned wider, and said, "You make me feel good, too." She walked over to the inflatable and looked inside. "Do those things help you go underwater?"

Paul looked and saw she was pointing to his fins. "Yes. They help me swim. And that's my diving mask. It lets me see underwater."

"I know. I've seen people using them." She hesitated, and asked, "Could you use that to find my boat?"

"We found your boat this morning. Don't you remember?"

"Yes, but I lost it again."

"You did? Well, I guess I'll have to find it for you, won't I?"

She nodded and pointed to the dive mask. "You'd better bring that."

Paul got up from the boat. "Do you think I'll need it?"

"Yes, it sank in some pretty deep water."

"Where did you lose it?"

She turned and pointed. "Well, I was playing over there, and it sailed away and sank."

"I see. We'd better find it together. Come aboard." He stooped, and she climbed into his arms.

Paul waded out into the ocean with Kristen balanced between his hip and left arm. When they were in water up to his pelvis Paul spied a flash of red on the bottom. "I think I see it, but I'd better check to be sure." He pressed the mask to his face and leaned forward in the water. He straightened up, and said, "I see it!"

"You do?"

"Yes. Would you like to see it too?"

"Yes, but I'm afraid."

"Don't be. I told you there's no monster down there."

Kristen clung more tightly to him.

"Here, I'll hold this mask to your face. Then I'll just barely lower you into the water. Okay?"

She nodded.

Paul lowered Kristen to the water. He held her with two hands so she could just barely peer beneath the surface. After a few seconds he lifted her up and took the mask away.

"How was it?" he asked.

"It was wonderful!"

"Did you see your boat?"

"Yes!"

"I guess we'd better get it then." Paul reached into the water and retrieved the boat. He began to walk back to shore when Kristen said, "I don't want to leave the water yet. I think I saw some fish down there."

"You did?"

"Yes. They were silver, and one was about this big." She held her hands about a foot apart.

"Wow! That must have been a whale!"

"Do you think he was?"

"Yes. Maybe we'd better check again."

"That's a good idea."

Paul walked into the waist deep water again and lowered Kristen with both hands, so she could see. The headache exploded out of nowhere. He stared at her curiously and started to release his grip. She sat up and squealed with delight. "I saw him again! He's right down there!"

She pointed to the water just in front of Paul.

Paul blinked his eyes as if coming awake. He felt his grip on Kristen start to relax, and grabbed her harder than before.

"Paul, you're hurting me!"

"I—I'm sorry. You started to slip." He looked confused. "I think we'd better go back to shore."

"Okay. Are you all right, Paul?"

"Sure. I have to go now," he explained, then deposited Kristen on the beach.

She nodded. "I had fun today. Can we do it again tomorrow?"

"I—I don't know. I may be busy, Kristen. I'll see you later."

The girl waved goodbye to Paul as he headed toward the diver's quarters.

*   *   *

The divers had built the dive shack under the supervision of Paul Kushe and John Reid, their resident carpenter and electrician. Everyone had pitched in and made short work of the dining hall, the dormitory, and this building where they kept their dive gear and extra supplies. It also doubled as a lab to clean and preserve any artifacts that they found. Barbara had taken over most of the building with her considerable tools and liquid-filled plastic vats. She was persnickety about order and cleanliness. Everything had its proper place. She was adamant about putting things away so they could be found later.

Mike rinsed the saltwater from his fins in the freshwater of a 40-gallon plastic can and wondered if maybe everyone was working too hard. He carried the fins inside while considering the possibility of taking a few days off.

Barbara stood at the workbench wearing a long white smock, tapping a cantaloupe-sized lump of conglomerate with a small, brass hammer. King was curled into a ball at her feet. When he saw Mike enter the dog sat up and thumped his tail with excitement. A quick glance was Barbara's only acknowledgment of Mike's presence.

Mike laid his fins on the workbench and knelt to greet King.

Barbara eyed him and the fins coldly. "Do I put my tools in your boat?"

"No, I'll put them away after I check on my pal." Mike lowered his voice and said to King, "I wouldn't bring any of my bones in here. You know how cranky some of these old biddies can get."

Barbara frowned. "Ha—ha, very funny, Mike. I'm serious about the fins though. You know where they go."

Mike rose and put them on the shelf where they were stored. He walked back to the bench and picked up a small, calcified lump, which had been found that morning. He fingered it thoughtfully.

Barbara glanced sideways, her tone softened. "I'm sorry. I shouldn't have snapped at you the way I did, but you know how I like things. I can't do my work and pick up after everyone, too! And you're the worst of the lot, Mike. Why do I have to keep reminding you?"

"I've wondered about that, too," Mike said. "Maybe it's because you like to talk to me."

Barbara laughed. "I doubt it."

Mike put the artifact down. "Hey, it's okay. Why should you be any different?"

Barbara set the hammer aside and regarded him curiously. "Different from what?"

"Paul. He just tried to end my diving career permanently."

"He did? What happened?"

"I'm not exactly sure. Everything was fine this morning. We had a good day—made some excellent progress. However, this afternoon he acted funny. I asked what was wrong, and he said he had a headache. Fair enough. I told him that I'd get someone else to take his place. When I turned to start the motor, he jumped me like a wild man. The next thing I know we're both in the water thrashing about. Somehow we got separated. Maybe the water broke his grip. I don't know. Then he looked at me amazed, and asked how we got into the water."

Barbara remained silent, listening.

"Paul swore up and down he didn't know anything about what had happened. The crazy thing is I believe him."

"I don't know, Mike. That doesn't change the fact that he tried to harm you. I wouldn't trust him."

"I have to. Any lack of faith might really send him off the deep end."

"So what are you going to do?"

"I'm not sure. Got any suggestions?"

Barbara thought a minute. "Couldn't you work with three divers instead of two? Maybe the presence of a third person would prevent another attack."

"Yes. I suppose we could. Nevertheless, that still shows a lack of trust. Besides, you're making it sound as if Paul can control his behavior. From what I've seen, he can't. Also, we don't have the manpower available to put three divers on a team."

"What's wrong with two teams instead of three?"

"We can't do that. We're understaffed as it is." Mike pondered the situation. "I've given this idea some thought. Maybe Paul's working too hard. Maybe we should take the weekend off."

Barbara smiled. "Mike, do you have any idea what today is?"

"Sure, Friday. Why?"

"The third of July. Does that sound familiar?"

"Tomorrow's the fourth," Mike said amazed. "Well, I'll be. I've been thinking about the excavation so much that I nearly let it slip by."

"It's an easy thing to do since the Jamaicans don't celebrate it. Out of sight—out of mind."

Mike nodded and smiled mischievously.

She glanced at him. "Come on, Mike. What are you thinking?"

"All right. How would you like to go to Montego Bay?"

"Oh, I'd love to. Who do I have to kill?"

He laughed. "Nobody. Look, let's do things right. Why not take a three-day weekend? Heaven knows we've earned it. The divers could use a rest, and you and I ought to do some research on that watch. What do you say?"

Barbara was delighted. "Yes—I say yes! Do you realize that we've been here for over a month and not had a glimpse of what the other tourists see? We haven't eaten a greasy hamburger or French fries—not seen ice cream in ages." Her face was aglow with the possibilities that a weekend in Montego Bay could bring. "Oh, I need to see the island so much! Do you think three days will be enough?"

"It should be. I suppose I could swing another day researching the watch."

"Could you?"

Mike smiled. "Yeah, I think so."

"Wonderful!"

"Here's the plan. I figure if we fly to Montego Bay—"

"We're not going to drive?" Barbara asked. "It's only four hours by car."

"I know, but with the narrow roads, and the crazy way people drive here. They drive on the left side of the road, remember."

"I guess you're right. We aren't in the United States anymore."

"No, we're not. Anyway, I figured we could fly to Montego Bay, hit the library right away, and then have dinner. You could have all the ice cream you want."

Barbara giggled.

"Sunday or Monday I'd do some diving."

Her smile vanished. "Diving? I thought this was supposed to be a break?"

"Oh, it is. However I'd never forgive myself if I didn't sample a few of the reefs."

She grinned. "You and your diving!"

"You're coming, too."

"Diving?"

"Yeah."

Barbara shook her head. "No, I'm not."

"Yes, you are."

"Oh no, I'm not!" Barbara folded her arms with a look of defiance.

"All right. No diving—no Montego Bay."

"You wouldn't."

"Try me."

Barbara grew quiet as she considered this.

Mike's tone softened a bit. "Come on, Barbara. I need a diving buddy."

"Oh, all right. Just one day though and only shallow!"

"Agreed. One day of shallow diving."

"I don't believe I agreed to this," she said, shaking her head. "I must be losing my mind."

"You'll love it. Trust me."

"Yeah, I'm sure," Barbara said, smiling dryly. "Mike, you know how much I hate diving. I barely made it through the underwater courses at school. That's why I got involved in the preservation end of underwater archeology. So I wouldn't have to make like a fish."

"I know, but you'll love this. The water's warm with hundred foot visibility, and afterward we can rent a car to see the city."

"Now that I'd like."

"I thought you would."

"Oh, Mike," she said suddenly remembering, "I just finished cleaning the watch. Would you like to see it?"

Mike nodded and followed her to the bench. She took the watch out of its freshwater bath and handed it to him. The case glittered in her slender hand. The blackened face had been magically transformed to the gleaming one that housed Mike's reflection. An intricate scroll pattern radiated from the center where the dials had been. "Truly magnificent," he murmured.

"I had to be careful cleaning the face," Barbara offered. "It's very thin metal and it had a terrible stain where the hands used to be. I had Mark take pictures before I removed them."

Mike suddenly set the watch on the table, an expression of fear and confusion on his face.

"Are you okay?"

Mike nodded. "I think so. I know this sounds strange, but why is it every time I touch that watch I get a headache?"

Barbara shrugged and both of them looked at the watch on the table. It glittered more beautifully than ever, but in an entirely new light.

Chapter 9

Dawn came slowly to the island and a peaceful stillness settled over the land while most things slept. The burgeoning jungle would be heavy with early morning dew. The moisture, which had collected on the broad leaves overnight, greeted the sun and sparkled like a brilliant cache of diamonds.

Mike Ryan was up early. He had gotten into the habit of watching the beautiful sunrise, which could be best appreciated from only a few vantage points. The west side of Chicago, where he had grown up, was not one of those vantage points. It was the same sun to be sure, yet somehow it was not the same. Maybe there was something about the water, or the atmosphere, or the magic of the sand under his feet, or a million other things. During his thirty-six years, Mike had found that a person's thoughts were molded by his or her experiences. Perhaps the sunrise in Chicago was every bit as beautiful, but he never recognized that fact because of what had happened before. Maybe the unpleasant things in his life had rubbed their dirt on him and tainted his memory.

As a teenager, Mike had hated to come home and find his father drunk and arguing with his mother. Mike had felt so sorry for her. She'd do her best, working every day, doing housework for the neighbors, trying to put food on the table and keep clean clothes on the three of them. Mike helped whenever he could. When he was sixteen he got a job after school selling shoes at Shoe World. It didn't pay much, but he was able to work twenty hours a week and give the money to his mother. She would insist on putting it in a college fund for him. His father rarely worked. As the jobs got fewer his drinking increased and so did the arguments. Soon he stopped looking for a job. Those times had been the worst. He'd get drunk early in the morning and heaven help Mike or his mother if they got in his way. Mike could not wait to get out of the house. When he had saved enough money he went away to college.

Mike recalled spring break during his junior year at Texas A&M University. He'd met a girl named Susan and being with her soon became the most important thing in his life. So much so, that Mike had lied to his mother. He said he could not come home on spring break because he had to help a teacher with a special project.

Five days after classes ended Mike learned of his parent's deaths. The campus police had come to his room to tell him that the police in Chicago wanted to talk with him. Mike broke the date he'd scheduled with Susan and caught a flight that evening. He learned the whole story from the police.

A few days earlier, when Mike should have been at home on break, his father had gotten drunk as usual, but this time he had a gun. He blamed his wife for his failures in life and swore that now he would get his revenge. The neighbors heard him ranting and raving and telephoned the police. A man who lived across the street tried to get inside the house, but the doors were locked. When the police arrived, they tried to talk Mike's father into surrendering. After twenty minutes of talking, he shot his wife in the head and turned the gun on himself. Mike felt that none of this would have happened if he had been there. Maybe he could have talked his father into surrendering and his mother might still be alive.

Mike's thoughts returned to the present, and he thought about pleasant things, like this weekend with Barbara. He longed to be with her, but was too shy to tell her. Perhaps she would be the spectacular sunrise that he needed so badly. He hoped she could make all his bad memories disappear.

*   *   *

Barbara stood naked at the window gazing out. The night had been hot, and she was unable to sleep. The early morning light touched Barbara's creamy skin and accentuated the high points of her breasts while her hair cascaded golden rivers down her back.

No matter how hard Barbara tried, rest would only come to her fitfully and in short spurts. Lately those spurts had become short, indeed. The last one lasted thirty minutes or so. After that, she lay awake for the better part of an hour. Her mind would not slow down enough to let sleep claim her; it kept replaying the events of the previous day and planning for the busy weekend ahead.

When the sun tipped the horizon, Barbara noticed a lone figure on the beach. The incredible beauty of the scene struck her—the crimson sun above a copper sea with a figure in silhouette. She knew instinctively it was Mike and rushed from the window to get dressed. King was curled up near her bed, his tail covering his nose.

The woman before him jerked Mike from his thoughts. Barbara stood with legs spread wide, blocking his path.

"A penny for your thoughts," she said. In her slender hand was a shiny copper coin.

Mike chuckled. "I don't think they're worth that much."

"So take my penny anyway, for good luck."

Mike took it and was silent.

"Aren't you going to tell me anything?"

"Nope!"

Barbara reached into her pocket and brought forth a shiny coin. "How about a nickel? Will that work?"

"Uh-uh, secret thoughts."

Barbara nodded knowingly.

They walked along the meandering high tide line. The arthropodal hoppers hopped, the crabs scurried, and downy brown and white shore birds played chicken with the sea. A wave would recede and an army of little birds would scamper forward, probing the wet sand with their long, thin beaks until the sea would gather strength again and make a rush for the shore. The quick little birds would beat a hasty retreat, one step ahead of the onrushing tide. When they had gone far enough, they would turn and wait for the water to flow back so they could start their serious game all over again.

Barbara spoke first. "I couldn't sleep, thinking about the trip and all. I saw you from my window and thought a bit of company might do us both some good."

"Thank you. I'm sure it will."

"So, you couldn't sleep either?" she asked.

"No, I'm an early riser. I like to prowl the beach early in the morning. It's invigorating, seeing the world fresh and new." Mike glanced at her. "It also gives me time to be alone."

Barbara stopped walking. "Oh, Mike, I'm sorry. If I'm interrupting, I'll—"

He smiled and took her hands—they were soft, like velvet. "No, don't go. I enjoy your company."

They started walking again; a myriad of small crabs scurried out of their way.

"Mike, why did you ask me to go to Montego Bay? Was it only to research the watch and go diving?" Barbara asked, brushing the windswept veil of hair back out of the way. She tucked it behind her left ear.

Mike stopped walking and faced her. "No, I asked you because I need someone who's qualified . . . and I guess because I like you."

Barbara nodded. "Then I'm afraid I can't go."

"What do you mean?"

"Just what I said."

"Why not?"

"Because," she said, and started walking again.

Mike had to rush to keep up. "Because why?"

Barbara stopped and faced him. "Because I'm only kidding, that's why. And besides, you're cute when you're angry. You get feisty so quickly."

Mike scowled.

"Oh! That's even better!"

She looked so inviting that Mike pulled her to him and kissed the laughter from her lips. Barbara was transported to a world governed by her awakening senses. She returned his kisses with a fervor that equaled his own.

They broke breathlessly. Neither of them spoke as they rushed to help each other out of their clothes. In less than a minute, they fell naked to the sand.

*   *   *

Afraid someone would discover them now that the beach was waking up, Mike and Barbara reluctantly got dressed and continued their walk.

"Mike, you still have not told me what you were thinking about this morning." Barbara's eyes were very wide and blue; her hair was lightly mussed.

Mike was at a loss. He wasn't ready to tell her about his family yet. "I told you," he said, suddenly defensive, "secret thoughts."

"So you did. Were they about me?"

He smiled a bit. "Typical woman. Thinks every thought a man has is about her."

"Aren't they?"

"Sometimes. Only this time I was thinking about the last five weeks."

"What about them?"

"Well, I was thinking about how busy they were. How we were all disappointed at first. No one said we'd have to build our own living quarters. They were just stacks of lumber. Remember?"

Barbara nodded slowly. Like she was giving this a shrewd appraising thought, and perhaps she really did not believe he had been thinking this at all.

Encouraged by her silence Mike continued. "We all pitched in and built the three buildings in a little over a week."

"That's because we were all anxious to start diving," Barbara said frowning. "I know you were."

"Uh-huh. Remember the feeling of satisfaction we had when we were done? It drew everyone closer together, knitted us into a team. It showed that we could accomplish whatever we set out to do. That's important, don't you think?"

"I imagine it is."

Mike found some dry sand above the high tide line and they sat.

"Is that all you were thinking?" she asked.

"Yeah, mostly. I was also considering what I should say in my report to the Jamaican National Trust."

"How often do you have to write one?"

"They expect a progress report every week."

"That sounds like a lot of work."

"It's not too bad if you keep up with it. I brought my laptop computer with me, so I make an entry at the end of each day."

"You brought a computer here?"

"Sure. Why do you ask?"

"The humidity is unbearable. Aren't you afraid of ruining it?"

"It never occurred to me. A computer's always has been a part of me. It's like my right arm. I'd feel funny without one."

Barbara glanced at his arm. "That's strange. I've never noticed it until now."

"Noticed what?"

"Your arm. It has a keyboard on it."

"Yes, it does. Want to see what I can do with it?"

She laughed. "Yes! What happens when I hit your 'enter' key?"

"Try it and see."

She poked his arm. Mike playfully grabbed her, and they began to wrestle. All of a sudden it was not a game anymore. The embrace grew passionate, and they fell back on the sand, kissing.

A small army of crabs worked the beach, hermits mostly. They paid little attention to the lovers. If it was not something to eat, it held no interest for them. They wandered every which-way, performing a peculiar, sideways waddling dance.

The storm seemed to come out of nowhere. The sky clouded up and wind driven raindrops pelted the two as they ran down the beach.

*   *   *

An overcast gray dawn touched the edge of Captain Anthony's world as he pushed the rusting handle of the pump while recalling the events of the previous afternoon. He had convinced himself that divine intervention had caused his dog to act the way he had. *Prince had a good idea, pretending to be drowning. His presence might warn the archaeologists of any danger.* Captain Anthony had not wanted to approach Mike on the beach because he was not sure how the man would react to an old black man talking about evil spirits. Captain Anthony filled the red, plastic water jug with cool water and bent to replace the screw-top lid. He was feeling rundown lately and knew it was not just early-morning sluggishness. Like everything around him, he was growing old. Last month he had turned ninety-one years old.

A few drops of rain stung Captain Anthony's cracked-leather cheeks as he looked up at the dark, lowering sky. He figured it would be clearing by afternoon and climbed the path to the lighthouse.

The white, cylindrical building stood one-hundred-ten feet high. It was the tallest manmade structure on the island when it was built; that was in 1833. The government thought it was a worthless relic, but the tourists knew better. To them it was quaint and picturesque. Its lightning rod dome was sheathed in classical-green copper, and the beautifully chiseled stone shone dazzling white against the blue sky above. The wraparound windows at the top were ringed by a black platform, and the glass in them sparkled in the sunshine.

Captain Anthony first met the "Old Girl", this is what he lovingly called the lighthouse, in 1937 when he was eighteen. He had been so proud because being a lighthouse keeper was an important job for such a young man. Then there were four other men to keep the lamp burning brightly and to rescue anyone from the ships that came to grief on the reefs. Anthony was sorry to say that there had been many of those, more than he cared to remember. He had often seen ships run aground and then pounded to pieces by the relentless waves. Sometimes the weather had been too rough to send a surf boat out to rescue the crew. Those times were the worst; when you could do nothing but watch men die and pick up the pieces when the storm had passed. In the old days they disposed of the dead as quickly as possible because of the heat. They had buried more than a few good sailors in the dunes behind the lighthouse.

However, those were the bad times. What Captain Anthony remembered most were the good ones. The times when the lamp burned brightly, and all of the ships would think of her as their friend. These days the enormous ships had deep drafts and plied the shipping lanes far north of here, in deep water. Not many ships came by anymore. An occasional trawler or pleasure craft would come by, but they were hardly enough to keep an old man company. Years ago the steamers that passed would toot a greeting, and the sailing ships would ring their bell or dip their flag. They were a friendly lot, nothing like the strangers today. They had known the light was there to help keep them off the treacherous reefs.

In the days before electricity, the light had required much tending. Following breakfast came the daily chores of polishing lamps and lenses, trimming wicks, filling fuel and other tanks to proper levels, and many other seemingly endless duties. If there had been a storm the day before, there was probably wind damage to repair, some shingles that had blown off the tender's house or a broken window pane that needed fixing. It was a never-ending job because Mother Nature could turn into a screaming witch at a moment's notice and vent her fury at the stubborn little lighthouse.

Thirty-five years ago, the government installed an automated light farther up the coast and retired his. They considered the old lighthouse unsafe and crumbling, but they held her in reserve in case the newer one failed. The new light had not failed yet, but Captain Anthony did not trust anything mechanical that had no human hand to guide it. *No, sir! A ship and her crew were too valuable to trust to a few wires and a motor.*

The government came by once a month to drop off supplies and Captain Anthony's retirement check, but they never intended on fixing the lighthouse. She was past her usefulness. "Expendable" was the word the manager of the lighthouse district had used. Anthony did not know what that meant, so he looked it up in a dictionary and was horrified by what he had found. *So the lighthouse wasn't needed anymore. Then neither was he!* Ever since then Captain Anthony had watched the new light in case it failed so he could light his lamp and save the day. That day had never come.

Captain Anthony opened a small enameled pot and poured some water inside. He would have tea and crackers while waiting for the storm to clear. However a few things needed to be done before he could sit. He must see if the automated light was lit and check the readiness of his lamp. More importantly, he must be alert for ships.

Captain Anthony picked up his binoculars and went to the green door that hid the rusting steel stairs that led to the tower. After a bit of climbing his leg muscles grew tired and he rested while gazing out the lower window. Through the fog he detected the dark outline of a ship. He became so excited that he continued up the stairs with renewed effort. The fog had cleared a bit by the time Captain Anthony reached the upper platform. To his dismay, he saw there was no ship. The fog—or his eyes—had played tricks on him. *Maybe the government was right,* he thought sadly. *Maybe I am too old. Perhaps both he and the light had outlived their usefulness. Maybe they were expendable after all.* Captain Anthony noted the hated automatic light to the east was lit. He put his binoculars away and went down the stairs.

Later, after the water had boiled and he had made his tea, Captain Anthony sat munching a cracker and thinking about the Dark One. His grim face was more drawn than ever. He hoped the young man would come soon because the Dark One was about to emerge from his tomb.

*   *   *

Paul sat at the dinner table contemplating the coming weekend. He did not have any plans and even if he did yesterday's fight with Mike changed all of that. He felt at odds with himself because part of him wanted to be alone to get some rest as he had been told, and another part, a mysterious one, wanted to continue working the site where he had found the watch. Paul guessed that that was impossible because he needed another diver to help with the dredge.

Paul saw Barbara and Mike walk in and help themselves to some coffee. He had never seen Barbara look so lovely or her cheeks so rosy. He wondered if Mike was responsible. The couple sat at the other end of the table. King, who had been watching the food on the table without making a sound, came over and sat near them. Mike ruffled the dog's ears, and King squeaked a happy reply.

Paul saw how cheerful they were and became more reticent. Mark Sullivan's irritating voice shattered his thoughts.

"Hey, Paul, have you got any plans for the weekend?"

"What?"

"I asked if you had any plans for the weekend." Mark was thin, about twenty-eight years old, with a large beak of a nose and thick rimless glasses.

"No. I haven't. Say, would you be interested in diving on that spot where we found the watch?"

"Well, I didn't have any plans, but I'd rather not go diving. My feet are so waterlogged I practically squish when I walk, and I'm still sore from lifting so many rocks."

Paul's smile deflated.

"I'll tell you what," Mark suggested, trying to reverse the effect of his last statement and find a companion for the weekend. "Why don't we compromise? How about if we do what you want today, then what I want tomorrow?"

Paul grinned. "Okay, you've got a deal!"

"Good. I want to go into town tomorrow and hit some of the antique stores. I understand you can pickup a good deal on some of the relics from the island history. Then I thought we could . . ."

Mark told Paul his plans for the following day and Paul nodded absently, his mind on other things. He was happy for the first time since they had found the watch.

The transformation was like magic. The once tranquil sky was a boiling witch's caldron of dark windswept shapes. Raging storm clouds seemed to threaten the island's existence.

Mark studied the lowering sky and shivered as a frigid wind attacked his bare skin like so many sharp-pointed needles. He stood on the beach wearing a blue swimsuit that had been perfectly adequate ten minutes before, but seemed woefully out of place now. "I don't think we should dive today. Maybe we should postpone it until tomorrow."

Paul remained silent, staring at the mountainous waves as they crested and fell on the troubled water. The sea had turned a forbidding slate-gray with alarming swiftness. He did not care about the rain or temperature because they'd be wet anyway, and the water would stay a warm eighty-seven degrees. What worried him was the surge the waves would create. To stay in one place in the water it was necessary to hold onto something solid and that left only one hand free to work the dredge. Paul knew he could not control it with anything less than two hands.

Cold, stinging rain pelted Mark. The northeast wind tugged at his hair, making it stand on end. "Maybe we shouldn't go in the water, Paul."

"Why? Are you chicken?"

"No, but the visibility would be terrible."

Paul smiled. "Come on, I'll buy you a cup of coffee while we wait out the storm."

The tropical storm had raged over the island spilling its rain and wind in chilling, temporary fury. The violent squall, typical for the Caribbean, swept in with a terrifying show of force, her winds high and whipping the sea into a frenzy. She struck hard and fast, leaving behind wet sand, high humidity, and murky water. When the potent Jamaican sun came out the island returned to normal so quickly that twenty minutes after the storm had left it was nearly impossible to tell it had ever occurred. The puddles of rainwater soon evaporated leaving only the turbid sea and a few broken trees to mark the storm's passing.

Paul and Mark loaded the inflatable boat and went to the location where Paul had found the watch. Although visibility was only a foot Paul swam to the bottom, nearly plunging into it head first and groped about like a blind man. Trying to get any work done was useless, so he headed for the boat. When Paul broke the surface, he saw Mark struggling to climb aboard the wildly bobbing inflatable.

Paul ripped off his mask. "What are you doing?"

Mark swung around, still clinging to the roller coaster boat, and peering through his fogged up mask. It was obvious he did not see Paul because he spoke to the vacant water to his right. "I'm not diving in this!" Mark yelled, clouding up his mask even more. The lens was chalky-white except where Mark's long nose touched the glass, cleaning it.

Paul knew that Mark was right, but decided to give him a hard time. "Don't be such a prima-donna. Besides, you promised me we'd dive here today."

Mark did not like to get anyone angry, especially the huge man in front of him. "All right," he said. "I'll go down when I clear my mask."

Paul had thought up a trick guaranteed to keep everyone in stitches for the rest of the summer. He would follow the dredge's hose down and wait until he heard the other diver's bubbles. Then he would home in on them and pull Mark's suit down. Paul nearly laughed aloud as he thought of Mark returning to the boat spitting angrily. "Okay, follow the hose to where we've been working, and I'll meet you on the bottom!"

A minute after Paul submerged the headache began.

Mark stripped off his mask, spit into it, and wiped the saliva around, cleaning the faceplate. *I don't like this. We've got no business in the water today*, Mark thought, angry with himself for giving in. He put the mask on, swam to the hose and went down.

The turbid water near the surface glowed an eerie green, but the deeper Mark got the colder and darker it became. He bumped into something in the gloom and drew back terrified, his arms churning the water. He lost all perspective and cart wheeled through the inky darkness not knowing which way was up or down. The only thing Mark was certain of is that he was scared and wanted to be out of this horrible place.

Mark felt something touch his back and froze.

It wasn't a hostile touch, but combined with the eeriness of his surroundings it possessed a certain menacing quality. Mark wondered if it was Paul. He prayed that it was.

Something brushed past him and Mark tried to penetrate the darkness with wide, terrorized eyes. *Perhaps it's a fish as blind as I am.*

There it was again—on the backs of both legs.

The frightened man turned to sweep whatever it was away and something tugged at his mask. He searched, but found nothing.

It tugged again. He frantically felt around his headgear.

Suddenly, something slammed into Mark from behind, sledge hammering the air from his lungs, and ripping the mask from his face. Cold water stabbed at his eyes and nose and a tremendous weight ground his face into the bottom. Mark was certain his nose had been broken, and he was choking on seawater and gritty sand that seeped into his screaming mouth. Seeping in also was the darkness. The darkness clouded his mind and turned his muscles to unfeeling rubber as he slipped into unconsciousness.

Chapter 10

⚓

John Reid looked through the dirty windshield of the rusted, blue Chevy pickup truck and keyed the ignition. The motor coughed several times, chugged unevenly, then sputtered and died. He pumped the gas pedal; it squeaked dryly, then he tried again. The engine started coughing and wheezing, the body trying to shake itself apart, then came to life spewing volumes of bluish white smoke into the gasoline scented air. Twenty years before the truck had been a rich blue. Now it was several lifeless shades lighter. The years of neglect and harsh elements had taken a brutal toll. The battered body was dust-covered and corroding away, returning to the ground from which it had sprung.

John was a mulatto whose enormous head encompassed the worst features each race had to offer. He nodded to Mike and Barbara as they approached from the left.

Barbara, looking smart in navy blue slacks and a white middy-blouse, opened the door to the truck. It made a rusty, hellish screech. Small flakes of rust rained from the bottom of the door onto her foot; the stuffy cab reeked of oil and old upholstery. She slid to the middle of the bench seat, lightly skimming the ripped seat cover. Mike tossed a tartan suitcase into the back, climbed in and slammed the door shut on the second try.

"Thanks for taking us to the airport, John. If I drove, I'd probably get lost and we'd miss our flight," Mike said, laughing.

John peered at them through sorrowful bloodhound eyes. His face was grim, as always. "I'm glad to take you."

The truck began to run rough, then died.

John frowned and shook his head. "I must apologize. My job with the government doesn't pay well and this poor truck must last a few more years."

Mike nodded. "No apology needed. I'm afraid being an archaeologist makes me somewhat of an authority on low paying jobs."

John dropped the truck into gear and looked straight ahead. *What did this damned American know about growing up poor in Jamaica?* John felt a need to tell Mike about how they came from different backgrounds and because of this he never had the opportunities the American did. "Perhaps you are an expert in your world, Mr. Ryan. What makes you and I different is you chose your job. I didn't have that luxury. Jobs are so few in the islands you have to take what's available and make the best of it."

John waited for a red car to go by before pulling out onto the two lane highway. "Let me tell you a story about my family."

"Sure. I'd love to hear about them," Barbara said, hoping that this break would give them a chance to discuss something else.

"My parents were farmers," he explained. "Look at the island and tell me how much farm land do you see?"

John gave them a second, then answered for them. "Very little. What's available is choice, and the price is high, especially for a black man married to a white woman. They didn't have much money, so they bought two acres of mountain side, mostly rock. It wasn't fit to grow much except a few bananas, mangoes, and a little coffee. Just enough to keep us from starving. We also raised chickens and goats which we'd take to market once a year."

John fished in his pocket for a cigarette, found one and lit it before continuing. "It was a lonely life for my mother because, when she married a black man, her friends deserted her. Even her relatives acted uncomfortable; especially when I was born. I hated to visit them and I imagine they didn't like it, either."

John sat back and reflected a bit. "Some of my father's friends deserted him, too. Not as many as my mother's, but a few. His family never abandoned him. The Reid's were warm, loving people. They made me feel wanted, like I wasn't a mistake. Because of them, I felt more black than white. When I grew older and tried to get a job, I saw other injustices. They weren't limited to my family, like I had thought earlier. They were aimed at most blacks on the island, especially the poorer blacks; the ones least likely to defend themselves. Through the People's Party I learned of an opening in the government's planning division and, with certain favors promised, I grabbed it. This is how I came to work for you. So you see, I really didn't choose my job. I merely took what was available."

Mike was about to deliver a scathing comment on how he did not have it so easy, when Barbara tried to break the tension by speaking first.

"John, what's the name of this road?" she piped with feminine curiosity.

He laughed tonelessly. "Just like all whites! Choosing to ignore my anger by pretending it doesn't exist."

"Oh, but you're wrong. I do care. So does Mike."

John paused to consider. "Of course, you do." His face broke into a large, unnatural grin. "You wanted to know about this road?"

Barbara nodded.

"These are the Palisadoes," said John. He put on his best smile, the one reserved for the tourists. "It's really unique. It's an alluvial strip created by centuries of sand and gravel deposited from mountain streams. The alluvium," he repeated, "joined a string of small islets and enclosed Kingston Harbor."

"You mean this was once under water?"

"Yes."

Mike wanted to clear the air between them and said, "John, let's get something straight. I didn't choose you for this operation. The Jamaican Government did. I don't know their reasons, but I assume you're to act as a watchdog. That's fine with me. I'm glad they sent someone to watch us so we don't steal any treasures," Mike's voice grew stern and he shifted in his seat to confront the startled driver. "I don't want any of this feeling sorry for yourself crap. I don't need it. That's your problem, not mine. Your Government put you here to find artifacts and to see if they should dredge the bay. I would like everyone to work together as a team." His voice softened a shade, but his eyes remained intense. "Maybe if we become that team, we can get this job done and make everybody happy. But if you start whining about how unfair things are, or anything at all, I'll stop work, and I won't start again until you're out of here." Mike thrust his face as close as possible to the driver. Sitting between them Barbara could only look timid. "Do I make myself clear?"

John was curiously calm, but his body was screaming. The veins on his forearms stood out like thick cords and the small brown hands on the steering wheel showed white at the knuckles. "Perfectly," he managed. To Barbara he asked, "Where shall I drop you?"

Flustered, she glanced to Mike for an answer, but he was staring out the window; no help. "Jamaica Air Lines would be fine."

John, grim as always, nodded.

As the swaying truck neared the airport, a 727 thundered low overhead. Everyone was grateful for the noise so they wouldn't have to say anything else.

*   *   *

John Reid watched Mike and Barbara disappear through the glass doors on the front of the terminal and considered their bitter conversation.

So the bossy American didn't want anything to foul up the excavation. How nice for him. How nice for everybody involved, everybody but John Reid. What if things didn't go as smoothly as planned? John tensed at the thought. *Since I'm one of the divers, I could see that they don't.*

His palms broke out into a nervous sweat. He needed a smoke. John took the pack of "Craven-A" cigarettes from his shirt pocket, shook a stick of ganja free that he had stashed earlier, and lit it. He smoked the joint continuously, inhaling it as he would oxygen. It had a soothing sensation, and he felt a pleasurable rush to his brain.

Through the curling blue vapor, he saw swarms of people passing in and out of the airport terminal. Some of them were businessmen, stepping from cabs with their briefcases and looking uncomfortable in their suits because of the heat. Others were tourists in tee shirts and shorts, sunburned and goggle-eyed, struggling with their luggage. John saw cabbies hawking rides and enterprising teenagers trying to carry the tourists' bags or offering to show them around the city for a fee. There were policemen, too, fixing everyone with their flinty, accusatory stares.

The end of the joint winked a seething yellow-orange eye in the shade of the cab. John thought, *Damn Americans! They tried to buy everything with their bloated Yankee dollars. Bloated, just like themselves!* As far as he was concerned they could keep their money and leave Jamaica to Jamaicans.

Thinking about the quarrel with his boss made John flush with renewed anger. Suddenly an idea struck him. He smiled with wonder as a plan magically unfolded before him. He started the pickup truck and pointed the dull blue hood toward Kingston. It was difficult to tell which was going faster, his racing mind, as it formulated the scheme, or the battered truck as it smoked on the Palisadoes.

*   *   *

Mike and Barbara entered the terminal with their luggage through the electric-eye-controlled doors. They were relieved to be inside where they could talk, and halted a few feet beyond the doors.

"I had no idea John felt that way," Barbara said.

"I didn't either. He seems to resent us being here."

"Nevertheless, his country called us in," she pointed out.

"Yes, but he probably feels there are deserving people here who could do the job just as well. You can't blame him for that."

"No, but what about this black/white thing? I think we may regret having him work with us."

"Perhaps."

"And by the way, thanks, pal."

Mike glanced at Barbara, a wide-eyed, 'I don't know what you're talking about' look on his face.

"You know what I mean. When you made that speech, I nearly stood up and cheered, 'Way to go, Mike!' Then you shut up and didn't say another word, left it to me. Some nice guy, huh?"

"I'm sorry. But I've had it up to here with foreigners thinking all Americans are rich and that we won't fight back."

Barbara looked troubled. "You mean you're not?"

"Not what?"

90

"Rich."

Mike became amused. "No."

"I'm sorry," she said. "If you're not rich, then I can't fool around with you."

"Why not?"

"A girl only has so many chances to land a rich husband; she can't afford to go out with every Tom, Dick, and Harry."

"My name's Mike."

"Same difference." She smiled.

The public address system announced that their flight to Montego Bay was now boarding at gate five and the couple hurried to the gate still bantering.

*   *   *

There were never any vacant parking spaces in downtown Kingston on a Friday afternoon. John Reid cursed his rotten luck as he drove up and down the crowded street in his sweltering truck. Even the brief rain brought no relief. The only thing that it did bring was the high humidity that turned his clothes sticky and uncomfortable. John saw a green Volkswagen bus on the other side of the street leaving a parking space. He swung a fast U-turn amid startled honking drivers, cutting them off and pretending not to notice as he pulled into the parking space.

John entered the large gray stone government building and crossed the high ceiling lobby to the chrome bank of elevators. He nodded a greeting to the stern guard while waiting for a car and basking in the air conditioning. For the nine years John had worked in the building, he couldn't remember ever seeing the man speak or smile. Perhaps he was the ghost of some long-dead guard who faithfully patrolled his post. The bell rang, the doors opened, and John stepped inside leaving the silent ghost to his lobby and his daily vigil.

John worked on the third floor as an electrical planner, but today he punched five for Planning Management. Because of his political connections he had managed to take a leave from his job and work in the harbor without a loss in pay. He was an archaeologist by avocation and loved the work.

John stepped off the elevator and walked down the deserted hall. His footsteps echoed his arrival on the freshly waxed green and black speckled tile floor. Pushing open one of the double glass doors of the Planning Management office, he walked past the receptionist to Bernice Holland's desk.

"Bernice," John said, interrupting her typing concentration in mid-sentence. Nevertheless, the dedicated woman felt obligated to finish the line and continued doggedly on until she was through.

She peered at him through thick bifocals, her hands poised above the keys. "John, what are you doing here? I thought you were going to be diving in the harbor all summer." Bernice raised her eyebrows, making her eyes look bigger than before. "Is anything wrong?"

"No. I just came back to see my best girl."

"Oh, you make me blush!" Bernice thought John was very nice and loved when he paid attention to her, like now.

"I also need to see the plans for the dredging of the harbor and the proposals."

Bernice's smile faded; she glanced around to see if they had been overheard. "John, you know they're confidential. Why do you want to see them?" Her voice was low, hardly more than a whisper, her eyes questioning.

"The head archeologist sent me to find out exactly how far into the area the dredging is going to extend," John lied.

Her expression remained fixed. "Why don't you go through the proper channels?"

"That would take too long. Besides, I didn't want to bother anybody. I know how things get Friday afternoon when everybody wants to leave early."

"But the proposals," Bernice challenged. "Why do you need them?"

John smiled, bewildered. "Whoa! What's with the third degree? I'm on your side. Remember?"

"But I'm not allowed to give—"

John interrupted her. "It's nothing complicated. We just want to ask the construction crews how deep they plan to dredge and what method they're going to use," he said, making up his story as he went along.   "That way we'll know if they dredge down to the archaeological layer. Frankly, I don't see what the problem is."

Bernice thought a moment. "I don't know," she said, shaking her head slowly. "I think I'd better ask Mr. Jacobson."

John could see that his plan was not working, so he quickly changed to another tack. "All right," he bluffed. "Jacobson's going to be very disturbed when his number one secretary had to interrupt his busy schedule to ask such a trivial question, especially when she's being considered for promotion to office supervisor."

"You heard that?" Bernice's eyes grew doubly wide. "You really heard that?"

"Yes." John glanced around and leaned close to whisper. "I'm not supposed to tell anyone, but Jacobson is really impressed with your work. He thinks you'd make a great office supervisor."

Bernice glowed with the compliment. "Well," she said, trying to sound business-like, "let me get what you need."

John watched as she stood, then walked toward the back. After five long minutes Bernice returned, motioning for John to follow her.

"I've found the plans and proposals and put them in a vacant office where you can study them," she said walking quickly, taking two steps for his one. "The telephone is disconnected so you won't be disturbed. Just let me know when you're finished, so I can put things away. And John," Bernice said, taking his hand and squeezing it, "thanks for telling me about the promotion. You're a true friend."

"Think nothing of it." John lowered his voice. "The only thing I ask is that you don't tell anyone, not even Jacobson. It's supposed to be a secret. He'd have my hide if he knew. In fact, don't even tell him I was here."

"Oh, he won't hear it from me. I swear!"

John's face broke into a genuine smile for a change. "I didn't think so."

The luxuriousness of the room amazed John. In the center was a black walnut desk of monstrous proportions which housed a considerable number of drawers that would take days, if not weeks, to adequately fill to one's satisfaction. The wall to John's right possessed floor to ceiling bookshelves in the same tasteful black walnut as the desk and contained orderly rows of books which all had the same red binding with gold lettering. The far wall contained three modern, bronze windows with fixed glass to keep the air-conditioned environment in. They displayed a breathtaking view of downtown Kingston and bathed the room in soft light. The two remaining walls contained several pictures of modern art; the kind critics rave about, but also the kind John looked at in amazement and wondered what the artist was thinking about, or if he secretly didn't know because he was high on drugs at the time. The most thought-provoking one was painted in fluorescent colors, using a palette knife, maybe a popsicle stick, depending on how artistically inclined the creator was. It was vaguely reminiscent of a waterfront scene except the water was purple and the sky was orange. Perhaps it was a picture of the harbor during a nuclear blast.

John sat in the comfortable, black leather chair and lit a cigarette while looking through the large set of plans. They were approximately two and a half by four feet in size, with three different widths of blue ink. The first showed the harbor divided into hundreds of fine lines from a grid which extended over the whole drawing.

John flicked his cigarette ashes on the carpet, smudging the rich beige pile a sooty black. He was pleased with himself for having gained entrance so easily to the heavyweight inner sanctum. John pushed back, placed his feet on the deep reflective surface of the desk and crossed his ankles. He remained this way, idly looking about, until he finished his cigarette.

Having ground out his cigarette butt in the upper left-hand drawer, John studied the plans in earnest. The proposed dredging was shaded blue, outlined in the heaviest ink and labeled in neat block letters. A two-thousand foot swath stretched from the outer harbor entrance to the proposed dock. There was also a notation that all shaded areas were to be dredged to a depth of sixty feet. John saw it would cut through the area they were working and put the new floor of the harbor twenty feet below the old street level. He considered this while lighting another cigarette, then leafed through the remaining pages. The drawings had the usual elevations, front and back, with a bird's-eye view encompassing the whole thing. The last sheet contained an artist's rendering of a busy dock with several large ships dwarfing the people below. One was a freighter unloading cargo and the other was a modern passenger liner with multi-leveled decks unloading volumes of smiling tourists.

John frowned. The ships using the new dock would bring more Americans. He could see them coming ashore, their pockets bulging with money and busily issuing orders, buying his country.

Next to the plans lay a blue folder marked "Proposals". Inside were eight detailed bids for the work from different contractors, five for the dock and three for the dredging of the harbor.

John looked through them briefly, and smiled. He had found what he was looking for.

Chapter 11

⚓

The sky had an orange, dusky glow as the sun prepared to set. The light peeped through the half-closed blinds, painting the rumpled hospital bed and the doctor with bold apricot lines.

Mark lay in bed imagining he must be dead because he remembered he had lost his air and mask and everything had gone black. *How could he be dead when his body ached? Dead people weren't supposed to hurt; that was the only benefit of being dead.* When he opened his eyes he saw an out-of-focus light. A voice was speaking to him from that light. Was it an angel? Mark had heard about people dying and being brought back to life saying they had seen a light at the end of a long, dark tunnel. He hoped this was such a light, that it was heaven.

"Mr. Sullivan, are you awake?" a man's voice asked.

A man? Where were all the female angels? Somehow, Mark did not picture it this way. Perhaps he was not dead after all.

"Mr. Sullivan?"

"Go away. I refuse to die and go to a heaven where all the angels are men," Mark said, trying to smile, but the pain from his swollen lips would not let him.

"It's good to see you still have your sense of humor," the cheerful voice said. "You had us pretty worried when you came in."

The image was brighter now. Mark could detect movement, and he felt for his glasses.

"If you want your glasses, they're on your night stand to the right of the bed," the light answered. "How do you feel?"

Mark probed for his glasses and found them. He placed them on the splint covering his nose, but they would not fit right and became crooked. "I feel as though an elephant sat on my head," he said, peering through the cockeyed lenses.

The light clarified and laughed. "I'm afraid you look like it, too."

Mark tried righting the glasses, but the pressure on the metal splint made him wince. "Thank you, Doctor?"

"I'm Dr. Weatherly."

"Doctor, I'm a little confused about the accident. Can you tell me what happened?"

"You don't know?"

"No. I know I was diving and nearly drowned. I remember my mask being ripped off, and being knocked down. After that, I don't recall a thing."

The doctor smiled. "Then perhaps I can help you a little. You'd be dead if it wasn't for your friend. I can't think of his name, but he's a big man with short blond hair."

"Paul Kushe," Mark offered with difficulty because he held the other man responsible for his accident.

"Yes, that's him. Well, he found you on the bottom, not breathing, brought you to the surface and gave you mouth-to-mouth resuscitation. He said that a wall or something caved-in. He was in tears when they brought you in. You're a very lucky man having him as a friend." The doctor stressed friend, and it rang in Mark's ears.

Mark nodded and wondered what had really happened.

The doctor folded his hands. "Would you like to see him? He's waiting outside."

Mark hesitated, unsure. "Yes," he finally whispered.

Everyone at the hospital had been friendly and concerned when Paul had come in with Mark. Since he wore only a swimsuit they had lent him a robe and slippers.

Paul smiled mechanically as a pretty, young nurse went by, her short hair and body bobbing to the rhythm of her walk. When he gazed after her, it was more from habit than desire. She continued down the hall, taking a right at the nurses' station. His eyes returned to Mark's door. He thrust his hands into the pockets of the terry cloth robe. It had been more than two hours since they had brought Mark in, and he was worried.

Paul thought back to Mark's accident to see if he could figure out what had happened. He recalled that he was going to pull a trick on the other man and went down the dredge's hose and waited. That's when the headache began and his mind went blank.

Paul tried to convince himself he was not responsible for what had happened. He remembered a noise, a low rumbling like distant thunder. Could that sound have been the wall collapsing? He recalled that he was feeling his way along the bottom when he nearly tripped over a body. He knew what it was by the feel of it: It had weight and was soft; the sensation was similar to kicking a hundred-pound sack of grain. When Paul knelt, he found his friend without a mask.

Paul tried to believe that the wall and not he was to blame for the accident. The waves from the storm must have loosened the stones that morning, and they had the misfortune to be in the wrong place at the wrong time. The falling stones must have knocked Mark unconscious and ripped off his mask.

Paul's face reflected doubt as he relived the accident again.

The door to Mark's room opened and a tall elderly gentleman walked over to Paul. He recalled the kind eyes of the doctor from the emergency room.

"Paul, your friend is awake. He wants to see you," Dr. Weatherly said, putting a slender, age-spotted hand on Paul's arm. "You can talk to him, but don't stay too long. He's been through quite a shock and needs rest."

Paul nodded and shuffled into the antiseptic-smelling room. A silent figure lay in bed, peering at him through puffy, half-closed lids. The face had a large, splinted nose and swollen lips. Mark's whole head seemed to be an angry, purplish-red color, kind of like blowing up a violet balloon and drawing Neanderthal features on it in red and black magic marker. Mark's balloon looked over inflated and about to burst. It trembled and words not air gushed out.

"Hello, Paul," Mark slurred through swollen, blood engorged lips. "The doctor said I owe you my life."

*   *   *

After Barbara and Mike landed at Sangster Airport they picked up their luggage and rented a pearl-gray Honda Accord hatchback. Although the car was less than five months old, it already had close to sixteen thousand miles. The engine made an annoying ticking when revved up.

They checked into the Jamaica Shores Hotel and received directions from the desk clerk to Instant Print, a one-hour photo service, to get the film of the watch developed. Next, they went to the Montego Bay Library and were directed to the Local History room by a young, dark-eyed girl chewing bubble gum.

The Local History room was divided into three sections. A dozen glass cases in the front contained old documents concerning the settlement of the island and some stone tools used by the Pre-Columbian Indians. In the center of the room was an information desk surrounded by eight wooden reading tables. Two girls and a boy sat at the nearest. They had a low, buzzing conversation going that was sparked with covert giggles and quick sidelong glances. Beyond them, the tables gave way to rank after rank of freestanding bookshelves.

Barbara and Mike paused a few minutes to gaze at the glass cases, then walked to the information desk. An old gentleman in a gray cardigan was sorting several stacks of yellow and white paper behind an old-fashioned wooden counter. He looked up as they approached.

"I wonder if you could help us?" Mike began. "I'm Dr. Ryan and this is Dr. Anderson. We're with a team of archaeologists exploring the city of Port Royal. We found a pocket watch among the ruins and need to verify that it was lost in the earthquake of 1692."

Mike opened the white envelope and produced the photographs Mark had taken. "The watch has the name Matthew Hudsen engraved inside the cover, and we'd like to find out more about him."

The man frowned and pointed to his left ear. "I can't hear. My hearing aid broke this morning," he shouted in a petulant voice, much too loud for a library.

Mike glanced around and saw a woman in a brown dress pushing a cart loaded with books. Barbara and he smiled at the gentleman behind the counter and walked over to the woman. The man shook his head, miffed, and went back to work.

The woman was returning books to the shelves and every few minutes she would purse her lips and mumble something. As Barbara and Mike approached she happened to see them. "May I help you?" she asked. The woman was in her forties, with brown inquiring eyes and a sharp nose.

Mike introduced Barbara and himself and explained their mission and the fact that the gentleman at the counter had been unable to help them.

She nodded. "Yes, that's Mr. Neil. His hearing aid went out this morning and the old codger's been testy ever since. He should be putting these books away—not me," she confided. "I should be at the desk. Why, he can't even hear the telephone. Whenever it rings I have to drop what I'm doing and rush to answer it."

"Oh my, isn't that terrible," Barbara agreed. "Could you help us then? We only have a few days and so much to do before we leave."

"I'd be happy to." The woman produced a paper and a pencil from a hidden pocket in the folds of her skirt. "How do you spell that name?"

Mike told her and she disappeared behind an area cordoned off from the public.

The librarian returned a short time later carrying a large folder. She opened it and handed each of them photocopies of the *Port Royal Journal*.

"Our old newspapers are on computer and when I entered Matthew Hudsen in the data base I found several references in these papers," she explained. "One is spelled H-u-d-s-o-n and the other is H-u-d-s-e-n. One article referred to a Matthew Hudsen, spelled with an 'e', as a wealthy man who was well thought of by the people of the town. It seems he had several ships that were used to fetch various goods for the city. Another article, dated May 1689, even speaks of a gold watch being given to Mr. Hudsen for his service to the city. It goes on to say that the watch was imported from the Netherlands, but it doesn't describe it."

She set the copy aside and picked up the other paper, saying, "Another article, dated August 1687, refers to a Matthew Hudson, with an 'o', and says that a meat-cutter arrived in town a fortnight ago and set up shop on King Street. I also ran across a paper from May of 1691. It says Mr. Hudson, with an 'o', was implicated in a series of murders, but the constable mysteriously took his own life before they could bring charges. He was replaced by a man named Victor Chapman. The May issue is the last we have."

"That's curious," Mike said.

"Yes, it is. The papers must have stopped a year before the earthquake. At least, we don't have them."

Mike studied the pictures of the watch and then the article. "It seems Matthew with an 'e' is the one we want. There's a deep scratch, and the writing is small," he observed, pointing to the enlarged photograph, "but it may be an 'e'." He passed the print to Barbara so she could examine it, too.

"Yes, the scratch starts above the 'd' then crosses through the 'sen'. It certainly looks like an 'e' to me. And what better gift for a shipper than a watch with a ship engraved on the cover?" Barbara looked at the others and said with conviction, "I definitely feel that this is the man we want and that is his watch."

The librarian beamed, pleased. "I'm glad I was able to help. I'm afraid I couldn't do much with the manufacturer. You could see if Dr. Henderson at the Montego Bay Museum might have some information."

The two got directions to the museum and thanked the librarian. She smiled as they left, then stalked over to reprimand the girls and boy for talking so loudly. Even poor Mr. Neil did not escape her scathing glare. He was oblivious, sorting papers in a world of his own, while the telephone rang off the hook.

*   *   *

Barbara and Mike arrived at the museum shortly before it closed at five o'clock. They hurried through the doors and saw a man in faded blue work clothes directing two similarly clad workers inside a nearly empty glass display booth. Mike asked where he might find

Dr. Henderson, but the man did not know. A custodian leaning on his broom overheard the conversation and showed them the way.

Dr. Bruce Henderson was not what Mike had expected. He was young, about thirty-five years old, and had bushy, sandy hair and a healthy moustache. His clothes appeared a trifle sloppy, but after watching him wield a pair of tweezers like a skilled virtuoso while squinting through a fluorescent magnifying lamp, Mike knew differently. Perhaps the man was eccentric, but he was not sloppy.

Dr. Henderson was so immersed in his work that he did not notice Barbara and Mike come in. They waited until the doctor was through. He was restoring a delicate figurine of a woman in a carnation-red gown atop an elaborately gilded baroque music box. Her left arm had been shattered and a piece had become lost, so the doctor had cast it in a white epoxy and was fitting the arm to the stump below her shoulder. After it had dried, he would paint it to match the right arm. The doctor finished, wiped his hands with a clean rag, and looked up at his visitors.

"Thank you for your patience. What can I do for you?"

Mike introduced Barbara and himself and explained their situation. He gave the pictures to the doctor while Barbara examined the music box.

"I've seen pocket watches like this before. The ship was a popular motif of that period, as were the stag, the eagle and many more."

Mike was encouraged. "The manufacturer was Karl Scheele. Could you tell us anything about him? Possibly, the years he would have been in business?"

"I can try. There's a book in my office that lists all the known watch manufacturers and their marks from 1500." The doctor extended an arm toward the door and led the way to his office.

Five dirty coffee cups and one stale donut hid among the scattering of papers that littered his desk. Journals and books overflowed the edges and several volumes had found their way to the floor. Dr. Henderson went to a built-in bookcase and scanned the rows of books.

"Ah, here it is," he called over his shoulder as he slid a large navy-blue book off the shelf, "*Timepieces and Their Manufacturers, Four Hundred Years, 1520 to 1920.*"

He sat, opened the volume in his lap, and pushed a mound of papers to one side of the desk. A few slipped over the edge and fluttered to the floor.

Dr. Henderson noted Barbara's reaction to the mess and explained, "I assure you the room gets picked up every evening. However, this desk is the local gathering place for half the staff. They have their morning coffee and their lunch in my office and whatever they have in their hand at the time ends up right here."

The doctor reflected a moment. "I don't see it as merely a messy desk, but prefer to think of it as an artists' collage that becomes complete by the end of the day."

"Very well put," Barbara said.

The doctor grinned his thanks and turned to the book's index. "Scheele—Sheele—here it is, Karl Scheele, page fifty-seven." He flipped to the page and read a bit.

"Okay, it seems our Karl Scheele was in business in the Netherlands from 1672 to 1708. The time span would place your watch during the earthquake. I'd say you have the genuine article there."

"It fits," Mike said. "The time is right. Even the newspaper said they imported the watch from the Netherlands. Then Matthew Hudsen, the shipper, is definitely our man."

Barbara nodded agreement.

Mike motioned to the book. "May I have a look?"

"Be my guest. I can run off a copy of that page, if you'd like."

"That'd be great!"

"No problem. Glad to be of service." The doctor placed a helpful finger on the page. "Here it is." He waited until Mike had leaned forward and looked at Barbara. He winked at her while talking to the other man. "It also has drawings of some of his designs on the next page."

Mike held the photograph to the book. "There's a slight difference, but they're essentially the same."

Dr. Henderson concurred, without looking away from the fair-haired beauty before him. "Yes, it shows they were engraved by hand."

Mike glanced up in time to catch Barbara scowling at the doctor, while he was gazing at her with admiring eyes. "Is there something going on here I should know about?"

"Oh no, I was just wishing I had an assistant as lovely as Barbara. Museums tend to attract the dried-up scholarly types."

When Mike was through looking at the book, the doctor left the room to copy the page. While he was gone, Mike looked to Barbara and said, "I'm proud of you."

"Why?"

"For showing me you're not a flirt."

"That's easy when you're in love," she said, then leaned over and kissed him.

When Dr. Henderson returned, Barbara and Mike thanked him for his help and left. Since it was after six PM and they had not eaten since they had grabbed some jerked chicken while waiting for their pictures, they decided to go to a restaurant rather than directly to their hotel.

The interior of the Clipper Ship restaurant had a novel scheme. Nothing had been spared to keep the diners in the finest of comfort while they enjoyed their dinner. Water surrounded the center of the restaurant, which contained a replica of a clipper ship. It had three towering masts that stretched to the forty-foot, sky-colored ceiling. Each mast was ringed at the base with tables of elegantly dressed people. On the right side of the bow was a lush, tropical rain forest complete with rainbow-hued, squawking parrots and inquisitive monkeys.

Barbara was striking in her caramel slacks and a cream-colored blouse, her blonde hair spilling over her shoulders. Around her neck was a flash of gold. A stunning seahorse dangled from a glittering gold chain.

Mike had ordered the surf and turf smothered in mushrooms and a bottle of white zinfandel while Barbara had a *filet mignon*, well-done, with a vegetable medley and a baked potato.

After several bites of her filet, Barbara lowered her fork. "When we were at school I never dreamed of being in the islands and eating in an elegant restaurant."

"Oh?"

"Uh-huh. I always hoped for something like this, but it seemed so impossible. I mean, here we are in Montego Bay, in a beautiful restaurant and doing the work we enjoy. It's all so unbelievable."

"It's not so unbelievable. You've worked hard to prepare for your career. You deserve it."

"Yes, I have. Only I'm afraid I might love this work too much."

Mike set his glass of wine down. "I don't follow."

"You know. I might become the stereotyped old maid who chose a career over a husband and a family."

"Hmmmm. I can see something wrong with that picture."

"Oh? What's that?"

"You forgot to mention the fact that you're a beautiful woman."

Barbara blushed. "Thank you, but I don't feel the problem lies in that area. Sometimes it seems I'm trying so hard to be a success that I get blinded to the fact that I'm a woman; that I have normal feelings and desires. My nightmare is that someday I'll wake up and find myself a lonely old woman. Maybe I'll become one of those dried-up scholarly types that Dr. Henderson was talking about."

Mike reached across the table and held Barbara's hand. "That'll never happen. Trust me."

"Don't be so sure!" Barbara said laughing.

Mike took another sip of wine. He had intended telling Barbara about his family and this seemed like the perfect time. Mike casually mentioned the deaths of his mother and father. He did not like to dwell on the unpleasant subject too long.

Barbara noticed the change that had come over him. He had the same brooding look she had seen on the beach that morning. It hurt her to think there was something between them over which she had no control. She suspected he felt guilty about what had happened and thought it might help by getting these feelings out in the open. Barbara started by asking a few questions, and Mike, aided by the wine and a sympathetic ear, revealed the whole story. When he had finished a great sense of relief washed over him because finally he had been freed from this terrible secret.

They ordered another bottle of wine and talked about his favorite subject, Barbara. About her childhood in Logansport, Florida, where she was the oldest of four children, her triumphs and defeats; about the time she had broken her ankle one week before the senior prom and had been absolutely shattered at the thought of missing it. Barbara recalled how her date had shown up two hours early with a bouquet of red roses and convinced her to get dressed so she would not miss it.

When they had arrived at the prom, her date set her crutches aside and asked her to dance. He practically carried her around the dance floor while the others looked on and applauded. It felt like she was flying and emotionally she was. It was so beautiful that she had cried.

She also remembered her duck, Quacky, an Easter present who had grown too big for her yard in the city. And how, at her parent's urging, she had taken him to a farm where he would have lots of room. She recalled being horrified when she went to see him only two months later and discovered that they had eaten him for Sunday dinner. That is when she had gone through her period of vegetarianism, which lasted a little over a year, about as long as her grief.

After Barbara had sniffled a bit, she and Mike finished their wine and drove to the beach. Once they had escaped the lights of the city, they found the shore dark and very nearly deserted. Although the sun had set an hour before, the residual light from the city was reluctant to leave the heavens. It glowed faintly violet as gossamer clouds hung over the western horizon. Faraway laughter could be heard from an unseen boy and girl.

Barbara and Mike took off their shoes, strolled hand in hand on the warm sand, and listened to the invisible sea as it crested and fell. A night bird called, and then was still.

Mike turned to Barbara; they kissed long and hard. When they separated, she took his hand and led him back to the car.

"Where are you going?" Mike wanted to know.

"I don't know about you, but sand got everywhere when we made love on the beach this morning. If we're going to fool around I don't want it to be anywhere near sand."

As Mike drove to their hotel Barbara teased him by unbuttoning his shirt and planting a string of wet kisses along his chest. When she undid his belt and pulled down the zipper on his pants Mike could not get to the hotel fast enough. He stepped on the gas and by the time he pulled into the parking lot she had released his manhood from the confines of his shorts and was kissing him. Mike melted down in the seat and busied himself with the buttons on Barbara's blouse. After removing her top, Mike imitated her kisses.

About the time he got to the top of her slacks, he realized there was not enough room in the front seat of the car, so they climbed into the back. He finished removing her clothes and remained motionless for a moment, drinking in her loveliness.

Their lovemaking was like nothing they had ever experienced. The passion seemed to reach new heights. It got better and better, until they thought they had reached a plateau, but then they were carried higher still. When it arrived, the release was electrifying and left the two totally drained. They lay motionless, locked in a lover's embrace, their sweat-drenched bodies entwined.

After a while, Mike murmured to Barbara, "Say, lady, how come we're making love in this car when we have a perfectly good hotel room?"

"Because this was spontaneous and exciting. Do you want to see my next surprise?"

"Yes, I can hardly wait."

"Come with me then."

They got dressed and hurried to their room.

Chapter 12

Mike awoke early and lay on the rumpled bed in the weak morning light. Barbara slept next to him. Her breathing was measured and shallow, her honey colored hair fanned out on the pillow like a golden halo. She was slight and delicate as a child. Barbara moaned softly, stirred and shifted a leg to a more comfortable position. The careless drape of the sheet pulled tight and dipped below one shoulder. He covered her again.

Watching her sleep Mike remembered how they had first met. He had been a graduate student in Professor Collingburg's archaeology class and was helping with the new students that swelled the class to overflowing every spring. Barbara had been one of those students. She was tall and curvaceous, but it must have been her high cheekbones that gave her that classic beauty. She looked like a flirty, sassy girl from a makeup ad who had come to life.

Mike had helped with the class three days a week, which was all he had time for. He tried to give equal attention to each student, but as the days stretched into weeks, he found himself slowly gravitating toward Barbara.

One day, when they were on a field trip and had roped off an area near the Brazos River to dig for Indian artifacts, Mike finally got up enough courage to ask Barbara for a date.

Barbara was trailing her gloved hand through the loose dirt in a sieve, looking for artifacts. After he asked her, she stopped her rummaging and looked up at him. "I can't, Mike." Barbara stood and pulled off her gloves. "I just got engaged." She appeared troubled, about both the engagement and why she felt a need to explain things to him.

"I guess I should have asked before." Mike forced a smile and turned to go.

"I'm sorry, Mike. Really I am."

Mike had quit helping with the archaeology class so he would not see Barbara. It did not help because try as he might she was constantly on his mind. He saw her from time to time between classes. She would smile and say, "Hi."

Mike found himself looking for excuses to pass by the archaeology room as it let out. If he was a bit early or the class was late, he'd find something that he absolutely needed to do right then, something important, like reading the bulletin board or maybe counting the number of tiles on the floor. When the door burst open, Mike would stroll through the corridor as if on an errand. He thought if he saw Barbara, she might say she had broken up with her fiancé and she was hoping he'd come along so she could tell him. Mike had hoped it might happen that way, but it never did.

After graduation, Mike heard she was still single. Trouble was she had moved back to Florida, and he had become involved with another girl.

When Mike had received the letter from Mr. Wilkens of the Jamaican National Trust, explaining the work to be done and asking if Mike could bring in some people, he became excited. This was his chance to see Barbara again. Now Mike's dreams had come true. Not only was he in bed with her, but they were in love, a love that a few short months before he would have thought impossible.

Barbara stirred again, hugging the sheet tighter, and moved back to the position she had occupied earlier. Mike brushed her hair from her face. It smelled satisfyingly feminine, and he kissed her forehead. She murmured a small sound of contentment and hugged him.

*   *   *

The shimmering sun painted the world in bright pastels and transformed the placid water in the harbor into a silver-white mirror. Occasionally a series of spreading ripples would shatter that mirror as fish grazed the surface in search of food.

Paul was worried sick. Had the wall collapsed, nearly killing Mark, or had he only imagined it? He needed to find out. If it was still standing, that meant he might have caused the accident when he blacked out.

He sat in the inflatable boat adjusting the straps of the backpack that held his scuba tank and tightened the buckle at his waist. He did not use the Hookah rig this morning because the compressor was too noisy and might alert the others.

After putting on his mask and fins, he leaned back and let the weight of the tank pull him into a back-roll.

The visibility had not improved beyond five feet, but Paul kept going. A dark shape appeared out of the gloom and lightened enough to reveal the familiar checkerboard pattern of the stones in the wall. Paul prodded the wall with trembling hands to see if it was really there and not an apparition of what had once been. It was solid and resisted an exploratory push. Paul hoped that this was not the same wall. Perhaps this was a new section uncovered by the storm. He searched the wall and determined that it was the same one where he had found Mark's mask.

Paul needed to make the wall collapse before the others discovered it was still standing. He shoved at the wall like a wildman, trying to make it topple. Time and marine growth had cemented the stones, and they would not budge. He planted his feet firmly on the bottom and used his shoulders to push. His feet slid back in the sand until he fell to his knees, but still the wall did not move. Paul picked himself up and looked around for something heavy. A rock lay partially buried at his feet. He dug it out and smashed it into the wall. In air the blow would have been tremendous. However, the water slowed it, and it only made a dull thump and raised a small cloud of silt. When the water cleared Paul saw the wall was undamaged. He backed up twenty-five feet, swam at the wall as fast as he could, holding the rock out front. He resembled a torpedo with a stone warhead, exploding on impact and falling to the bottom. Paul shook the fuzziness from his head and charged repeatedly until the wall shattered.

His fingers torn and bloody, Paul slouched and breathed huge quantities of air at an alarming rate. After his breathing had slowed, Paul inspected the scene. A metallic object protruded from the sand. He grasped the goat's head handle of an old dagger and worked it free from the bottom. Next to it was Mark's mask. It lay partially buried, still attached to coils of white air-hose stretching into the gloom. Paul set it on the rubble from the wall and shattered the faceplate with the butt of the dagger. Then he placed a large rock on the hose, kinking it. Putting the knife in the waistband of his suit, he surveyed the scene before him. This was the way Paul had envisioned it all along, the way it should have been.

Pulling the inflatable ashore, Paul found young Kristen waiting for him.

"Hi, Paul. Can we go in the water today?"

"No, I can't. I'm very busy," Paul said, afraid of being alone with the young girl, afraid of what he might do to her if the headache came.

The girl looked forlorn, then brightened. "Maybe I can help you."

"No. I don't think that's a good idea. I have to go now. Bye, Kristen." Paul turned and began walking to the dive shack. As he went away, his hand brushed the handle of the dagger he had stuck in the waistband of his swimsuit; he grimaced in pain as the headache flashed inside his brain. He turned around and called to the small girl as she was walking away. "Kristen, wait!"

The girl spun around hopefully. "Yes?"

"I just remembered. I lost a diving weight in the water when I was pulling the boat ashore. Would you help me find it?"

"Oh, yes!" she cried, and came running over.

"Okay." Paul lifted the young girl up and retrieved his diving mask from the boat. "I think I lost it right over there," he said, walking into the water.

Soon the water was over his waist, and Kristen hugged his neck tighter. "The water's getting very deep. Is it much farther?" she asked.

"No, it's right around here. Why don't you put on the mask and look for it?"

She did, and he lowered her mask-covered face into the water. After a few seconds, she sat up.

"I don't see anything but sand. Let's look over there."

Paul moved to where she pointed. She dipped her face into the water again. He surveyed her frail body and thought how easy letting go would be and letting her drown. Satan would be pleased with such a fine offering. Paul shook his head. *What am I thinking? I am hardly religious and I am thinking about Satan?* As strange and absurd as the thought seemed to him, he began to forget thinking about Satan almost instantly and in moments it was as though the thought never was.

Kristen sat up, and shook her head. "I still don't see it, but I saw another whale."

"You did? Terrific!"

"Let's look over there," she said pointing.

"Okay."

Paul waded over to where she wanted to go. She lowered her mask-covered face into the water again. When he released her, Kristen raised her head, screaming. The sudden, unexpected sound broke the trance Paul was in, and he grabbed the girl and lifted her out of the water.

"You scared me!" she cried.

"I'm sorry. You slipped." He hugged Kristen to his chest. "I think we should go back now. I don't really need that diving weight after all."

"No! I don't want to go yet!"

"There are things I've got to do," Paul explained, afraid of what might happen if they stayed.

"But I think I saw a whale. He was much bigger than the one yesterday."

"That's wonderful, but we need to get back." He turned and began walking to the beach.

She hugged him tighter and flashed her brown eyes at him. "Please! Can't we stay for one more dive?"

Her little girl charm had a devastating effect on his resolve, but he was determined. "No. I need to get back, and your mother is probably wondering where you are."

When Paul was not looking, Kristen dropped the diving mask. "Uh—oh!"

"What happened?"

"I dropped your mask. I'm sorry."

Paul stopped walking and assessed the situation. He needed that mask. It was the only one he had.

Kristen pointed behind them. "It's right over there."

"Okay. One more dive to find my mask, but that's all."

She jiggled in his arms with delight and pointed to the spot where it sank.

The headache descended over him like a black fog, taking him away to a place of oblivion and bringing Matthew Hudson back to life. In one swift motion, Paul's left hand pushed Kristen under the water while his other hand retrieved the dagger from his waistband and plunged it into her chest. When he felt the dagger go in to the hilt, he ripped downward and split her chest open, letting the water invade every cavity so her body would sink. The water in front of him churned as the girl struggled, but it was over in less than a minute. Paul released her in the red tinted water and she drifted to the bottom.

*   *   *

John Reid shielded his eyes from the strong Jamaican sun looking first at the piece of city hall stationery, then at the brilliant lime-green building. The paper read Caribe Dredge and Dock, 5227 Ocean View, but the faded address plate on the building read 52 7. The building to the left was a small flamingo-pink structure with burgundy shutters, a corrugated tin roof, and equally faded numbers that read 5231. To the right of the green building was an empty lot covered in long, shaggy grass that nature was trying to reclaim, but an occasional visit from a lawn mower would not let her. By process of elimination the green structure had to be the one he wanted.

It was a simple cement block building with a flat roof and a gray steel door with aluminum-framed windows to the right and left. Finding no bell, John knocked on the door.

The door flew open revealing a large, stocky man with a red beard and intense blue eyes. He appeared ill tempered and John wondered if he had chosen the right company to deal with.

"What can I do for ya?"

"Is this Caribe Dredge and Dock?"

"Aye, I'm Pat O'Reilly, the owner. And who might you be?"

"I'm John Reid. I'm with the Kingston Planning Division. I'd like to discuss the bid you made for dredging the harbor."

"Would ya now? Well, come in out o' the sun and let's talk," he said, clapping the smaller man on the shoulder.

The two stepped inside the air-conditioned office. O'Reilly sat on a corner of the cluttered, rubber-topped desk. His powerful arms were covered with thick, fiery-orange hair, and he wore scuffed high-topped boots, gray work pants, and a black T-shirt that read "Cool Runnings".

"As I said before, Mr. O'Reilly, I'm with the city's planning division. My job is to work with the archaeologists in Kingston Harbor. Naturally, my findings can have a great influence on whether the channel is ever dredged. Caribe Dredge and Dock," he continued, peering at his notes, "submitted a bid for the dredging of the Harbor. Are you familiar with that bid?"

The man sat across from him with arms folded; even the curly red hair that covered them appeared rebellious and wiry. They corkscrewed out at different angles refusing to lie down. Pat O'Reilly measured the worth of the little man seated before him. He wasn't impressed. "Aye, I made it myself."

John Reid's eyes glittered when he saw the other man hunch forward, listening. "I can see that you'll get the contract if certain conditions are met."

O'Reilly considered this for a moment. The contract was a rich one. Nevertheless, he didn't care for this little man with his nervous eyes and weak chin. He shook his great head, trying to read the other man's expression. "I dun know. I bid that job cheap. If yer wantin' a pay off, I couldn't give you much."

"That's the problem. Your bid is too cheap. I know from experience that when there are three bidders for a job, it'll go to the middle one. The city always rejects the highest one as too costly. The low is usually thrown out because it may contain inaccurate bidding and the contractor could cut corners and do an inferior job. The man who made the middle bid is the one who'll get the work. I think if you were to raise your bid by," he paused, his eyes looking off into space and then continued, "two hundred thousand, I can guarantee you'll get the job. That'll leave eighty thousand for you, eighty thousand for me, and the other forty thousand will be used to pay off the right people at the right time."

The bearded man broke into a broad, toothed smile, his eyes shrewd, giving him the appearance of a cunning pirate. "Aye, it all sounds good, and it may well be. But why did you pick me? And why do I need you? What if I just raise my bid and cut you out?" O'Reilly asked.

"There were seven bidders for the dredging," John lied. Only three had actually made bids, but he wanted to make the contract seem harder to obtain. "I have a feel for these things. I checked the others and they weren't hungry enough. Since you were the lowest bidder, it left enough room to raise the proposal."

John smiled and addressed the other question. "You need me to help smooth the road so you'll get the job. I'll keep the National Trust in check by seeing that nothing of value is found in the harbor and grease a few palms. Since you're in the construction business, you know how everyone who issues work permits has his hand out. I am of value because I have the expertise of knowing whom to see and what it will cost. Do you understand?"

"Aye. But what if the government decides not to go ahead as planned?"

John Reid waved a hand in dismissal. "The business men in Kingston would never stand for it. They're very persuasive because they stand to make a lot of money if the harbor is dredged. The tourist trade alone represents tens of millions of dollars. The government will get its share, and believe me, when it comes to money, they can be as ruthless as anyone. Besides, whoever is the least bit political is jumpy as a cat before an election. They don't want to offend anybody, especially a group as powerful as the Merchants Association. I also have an ace in the hole," he confided. "Don't forget. I work in city hall, and I know all the right people. How they think and what they will accept. More importantly, I understand what they will be willing to overlook for a price."

O'Reilly looked doubtful. Perhaps he was being set up for a police sting intended to snare businessmen like himself. Maybe the incumbents needed a law-and-order crackdown, something to look good before the election. Still, this was a bargain. "I might be interested in making a deal."

"Good. I'll handle everything. All you have to do is raise the bid and play along. Do you have any questions?"

O'Reilly sat analyzing the information, then stared at Reid with piercing, blue eyes, eyes that warned not to cross him. "No questions. Just a couple o' things that need to be said. If this is part o' some police crackdown, or you're not who you say you are, I'll tell you this right now: they might arrest me, but I'll track you down and feed your gizzard to the fishes!"

Reid swallowed hard. "Of course it's not."

O'Reilly considered him for a moment. "Okay, but I'll raise the bid by two hundred, fifty thousand. A hundred and thirty for me."

"It's a bit steep, but that shouldn't be a problem. Then we have a deal?"

"You bet we do! Welcome aboard, Mate," O'Reilly said, holding out a huge hand.

Chapter 13

The sparkling ship moved easily through the billowing sea with the comfortable self-assurance only a large vessel commands. Her clean lines seemed to smile as she plowed through the advancing rollers, the oyster-white bow high and proud, glistening with spray and begging for more. Her name was splashed on either side of the bow in red cartoon letters and proclaimed *Captain Crunch* was responsible for parting the surging waves.

Although he was only twenty-six years old, Kent Maxwell handled the sixty-five foot craft extremely well. He knew how to ride the troublesome waves—bow on with a little power, just enough to break through the surge. His active blue-gray eyes looked at the GPS while his hands clutched the spoked wheel and the wind ruffled his sun-bleached hair. He was trying to find a little-known section of a reef system called Kent's Castles. All good charter boats on the island had their secret locations with which to lure customers, and this was one of the best. Kent jockeyed the boat around for ten minutes before his first mate released the anchor.

Mike Ryan put on his scuba gear, only half listening to the captain describing the dive site and the procedures everyone should follow.

Mike finished putting on his gear and checked Barbara's progress. She was struggling with the straps of the rental buoyancy compensator, and he came over to help her. After she had it adjusted to her satisfaction, they headed for the boat's transom and the water.

The warm water was so clear that they could see the reef sixty-five feet below them. As they neared the bottom, a huge school of silver baitfish swam a ballet pattern seemingly choreographed to silent music only they could hear. They were sheer wonder to watch. Not one fish turned the wrong way or made the wrong move. Their silvery sides caught the light and reflected it, creating a large shimmering mirror with a thousand eyes.

Coral fairy castles, submarine towers, and Hobbit hideaways appeared everywhere. Each housed a swarm of colorful fish and little sea creatures that peeked at the divers secretively. Surely if there was an enchanted land, then this was it. The baitfish ballet approached and seemed to pirouette as the leading edge parted and then flowed around the divers as if they were rocks in a stream. The fish glittered like so many snowflakes and were gone, perhaps to enthrall other sections of the reef.

Soon the underwater fairyland sloped into the perpetual darkness of the abyss. The drop-off was lined with an incredible variety of corals and sponges that defied imagination. They enticed Mike with their beauty, beckoning him to explore their magnificence. He swam over the edge dragging Barbara along. The fantastic undersea growth around them captivated them. It was similar to being in a time warp. The deeper they went the larger things became. Even the fish browsing all about them seemed bigger, some sort of prehistoric relatives of the smaller fish above.

Mike looked from the luminous dial of his watch to his depth gauge and realized they were too deep. He signaled Barbara that it was time to head back. With great reluctance, they turned around and began their ascent. Barbara glanced up and saw their exhaust bubbles break the ranks of a troop of blue chromis, scattering them in disarray. The fish swam around the divers, regrouping on the other side so they could compete with the silver baitfish for first prize in the underwater ballet. Barbara and Mike finned upward, storing up memories of the magnificent scene around them. They came up the anchor line and swam to the back of the boat.

The captain helped the couple aboard and assisted in removing their tanks.

"Did you enjoy your dive?" Kent asked. The question was more of a formality than anything else. He already knew what kind of dive it had been from their faces.

"Yes, it was incredible!" Mike said.

"Everything was so beautiful," Barbara added.

"I'm glad you enjoyed it. I knew you'd like this spot." Kent finished helping Barbara off with her tank and came over to give Mike a hand. "Where are you from?"

"The States. I live in Chicago and Barbara's from Florida."

Kent nodded. "Are you enjoying your vacation so far?"

"We're not on vacation. We're doing an excavation at Port Royal," Mike explained.

Kent flashed a knowing smile. "You're Mike Ryan, aren't you?"

"Yes, but how did you know?"

"I read all about you and the excavation in the paper. I grew up near Port Royal, you know. Ever since I was a kid I've always wanted to dive there for treasure," he said, staying alert for other divers. "Too much sand for me; everything's buried."

"You sound like you speak from experience," Mike said. He found his gear bag, opened it wide and rummaged around.

"A little. I poked around very close to your excavation."

Mike sat on the gunnel, drying his hair with a towel. He told Kent briefly of the excavation's progress.

"This is the first chance we've had to do some recreational diving since we came to the island," Mike explained, tossing the damp towel onto his shoulder. "The water around Kingston is so boring. It's got very few fish and absolutely no coral."

Kent gave Mike an appraising look and glanced at the other divers around them. They were too busy talking about the dive or stowing their gear to pay any attention to what he was about to say. "I grew up in Kingston," he said softly, and the wind ruffled his shaggy hair, "and there's a place to dive which I think you'll like. If you're interested we'll have dinner and talk."

"Sure, I'd like that."

"Good. You won't be sorry." Another pair of divers had surfaced and Kent went to the transom to help them aboard.

Mike dragged the towel from his shoulder and went to dry Barbara's back.

It had taken three heaping platters of grilled mahi-mahi, fried conch fritters, and wild rice with steamed vegetables to satisfy their ravenous appetites. There was something about the sea air and diving that made your stomach seem larger and harder to fill. Mike and Kent sat on the terrace of the hotel, sipping beers and talking about the excavation. Barbara was enjoying her second glass of iced tea.

"About seven years ago, when I lived in Kingston," Kent began, draining the pitcher into both his and Mike's glasses, "I got an old twenty-two foot wooden boat. It was nothing special. It had a ninety-five horse outboard. The hull leaked a little, but it was the answer to a dream for me. I loved to dive, so I figured I could make a living by taking out diving charters."

Kent took a swallow from his beer. A waitress moved in silently as a ghost and replaced their empty pitcher with a full one. Mike cast an inquisitive eye at Barbara. She was stroking her hair and seemed a little too interested. Did the story or the teller spark this interest?

"I think I dove every spot within a five-mile radius of the city," Kent said, "and always found the bottom to be flat and boring. A few spots quickened the pulse and made you believe you were on the verge of discovering something incredible. Some small patches of coral with lots of snails and lobster, enough to keep you busy and take your mind off exploring for a while. That's the way the sea is, you know. It gives up just enough to tease you into thinking you might have something, then it snatches it away just as quickly.

"One day," Kent continued, "I took a bearing of two hundred degrees from the Kingston Harbor light and went past my usual five miles. At twelve and a half miles, I noticed a darker blue on the horizon. I saw that area was roughly circular and toward the center was the most intense blue-black. I knew that color meant deep water and that I had found a blue hole!"

Since no one said anything, Kent asked, "Do know what a blue hole is?"

"I think so," Barbara said. "Correct me if I'm wrong. It's an underwater sinkhole whose sides consist of porous limestone."

"That's right. You get an A in geology," Kent said.

"I thought Jamaica didn't have any blue holes," Mike said.

"I did too, but there it was. When I dove, I found the hole was ringed with coral and huge sponges and this puzzled me. I had always thought that such large coral didn't exist so close to the southeastern corner of the island. The only explanation I could think of was that a subterranean passage must have been providing nutrient-rich water to sustain the incredible growth. I could feel such a current rising from the depths."

"It must have been a chimney effect," Mike observed, and the others turned to look at him. "The movement of the water over the surface of the hole creates a sort of up welling which brings in water from miles away."

"How deep was it?" Barbara asked.

"I don't know. I dove to one hundred fifty feet, but the hole continued to drop."

"Weren't you afraid?"

Kent laughed. "No, I've gone down to two hundred feet before. If you've got confidence in yourself, there's no reason to be afraid. Besides, the water was so warm and full of life that you just couldn't believe you were in any danger."

Mike poured himself another beer. The foam ran down the sides of the glass and onto the table. Mike did not like Kent. He was too pretty with his blond hair, deep tan and flawless white teeth. He exuded a fresh, healthy glow like maybe he should be selling vitamins or toothpaste. Mike looked at Barbara and Kent, and thought, "They look like they belong together, a real-life 'Barbie and Ken'."

"It's a fantastic dive," Kent promised. "I've never seen such an incredible variety of sponges in all my life. There's even a barrel sponge big enough to sit in."

"It sounds thrilling! Have you taken any pictures?"

"No. My eyes are my camera, and my memory is the film."

"You ought to invest in an underwater camera. There's so much to see, to remember," she said, and then brightened. "I know! You could start a book and show it to people, so they'll come on your charters. It'd be great for business."

Kent smiled politely.

"You should, I'm serious!"

Mike emptied his glass and slammed it on the table loudly. "Oh, you really should! I'm serious!" he said, mocking Barbara.

She glared at him.

"Do you really believe him?" Mike asked. He didn't care if the story was true or not. He just wanted to ruin Kent's credibility in her eyes. "I surely don't. How come we've never heard about this before? And if it's as big as he says, then shouldn't it have been spotted from the air. Manley Airport's only fifteen miles away. How come nobody has ever reported it?"

"I don't know. I've often wondered about that myself," Kent said.

There was an awkward silence while everyone thought of what to say.

Finally Mike spoke. "You know what I think. I think he made up that story to entertain tourists and impress pretty girls. All he wants, Barbara, is to get in your pants."

"Mike!" Barbara blurted.

Mike ignored her and turned to Kent. "She doesn't believe me. Why don't you tell her?"

"Everything I've told you is true. I'm also insulted by what you said."

"I didn't mean to insult you," Mike said sloppily, fingering the rim of his glass. "I'm sorry if you feel that way. I just meant that you're lying."

Kent dove across the table and slammed Mike in the mouth with his fist. Mike flew off his chair, and Kent scrambled on top of him.

The taste of blood jarred Mike into sensing his vulnerable position. He stabbed his foot at the other man's mid-section, causing him to flip into the table behind.

Mike hustled to his feet and smashed Kent with a solid uppercut as the man was getting up from the floor. It knocked him back, causing him to lose what little balance he had and sent him crashing into another table. Mike dove on him, trying to hammer the pretty-boy nose to the other side of his face.

The two rolled on the floor trading punches while Barbara stamped her feet, screaming for them to stop. She went unnoticed by the combatants, but the three of them gathered a ring of curious spectators. The men fell off the deck onto the sand where they staggered to their feet and came at one another again. They were growing tired and their punches either missed wildly or landed an ineffective, glancing blow.

Mike squared his shoulders, struggling to hold his leaden arms up, while Kent circled to his left. Both men threw a wild right that missed and then fell dead tired into each other's arms. Kent began to laugh from utter exhaustion while Mike barely held on to him. Soon he was laughing, too. They talked several minutes, clapped one another on the back and walked over to Barbara.

She stared at them incredulously. A moment ago they were trying to bash each other's brains out and now they looked like long lost buddies.

The men smirked at each other when they saw her confused look.

"I don't believe what I'm seeing! Are these the same two men who stormed out of here, trying to knock each other senseless?" She was happy to see them become friends, but was puzzled by the mysterious turnabout. She attributed it to the childish thinking of the male mind.

"We got so tired we couldn't fight anymore," Mike explained breathlessly, his chest heaving, and his mouth bloody, "so we figured we'd better become friends and get a beer."

They looked like small boys who had been naughty and Barbara was tempted to treat them as such. The sand clung to their bodies making them appear as if they had some rare tropical disease. She smiled. "Okay, you're forgiven. But I don't want any more fighting. Understand?"

They nodded.

Barbara shook her head, drew her lips tight to keep from smiling. "You two are the dirtiest, sorriest sight I've ever seen!" Then she softened a bit. "But both of you look so funny, you're cute."

The men grinned, nodding to each other, and grabbed her by the arms and legs. They carried her shrieking to the water, and tossed her in.

Barbara got to her feet sputtering, pretending to be angry. She was glad to see them working together; at least they weren't fighting. When the men turned to go, she chased after them splashing and squealing until they had enough and tossed her in the water again.

Later, all three sat on the edge of the deck toasting each other for their harmonious personalities. The men succeeded in talking Barbara into having a few glasses of white wine.

She became talkative and light headed after the third glass. "What I want to know," she said, waggling a crooked, demanding finger, her eyes crossed slightly when she became a bit tipsy. "How come you two became such good friends after the fight? Doesn't make sense."

"It seems Mike was worried that I had ideas about you and me. When he found I didn't, everything was pretty much settled." Kent touched his jaw reflectively. "At least, I think it was."

Mike smiled and poured Kent another beer.

"I also told Mike I'd show him the blue hole if he'd let me work the excavation for a few days."

Barbara was confused. "You mean you're willing to go back with us just so you can work?"

"Yes, something like that. I also had to promise I wouldn't make a play for you."

She looked surprised. "You mean you two bartered for me like I was a cow?"

"A prize cow," Mike corrected.

Barbara spun on him. "What gives you the right—the gall, to think you own me?"

For the first time that evening, Mike was speechless.

Barbara liked to think of herself as an independent woman. Hadn't she gone to college and made her mark in a man's world? Still the idea of being possessed intrigued her. It made her feel wanted. She felt warm and couldn't decide if it was the wine or the thought of being someone's property that increased her temperature so.

"Don't I have something to say about this?" Barbara pouted. "I was hoping to go to you, Kent."

Mike considered this for a moment. "Well, I guess she's all yours. I'm too drunk to stand up, let alone fight."

"No, Mike, I couldn't possibly. Not after you've invested so much time in her."

"No, I insist."

"I can't take her. You found her first so she's all yours."

Mike was struck with the truth of the other man's words. "You're right. I found her first, so she's mine to give away, and I give her to you."

The trading went back and forth, until they agreed that Mike had found her first and therefore, he had first claim. They also agreed that when he died, Barbara would go to Kent. It was a pact made by two friends who had too many beers in too short a time. When they were through sketching out the details, it was after two in the morning. Barbara was curled up on a beach towel asleep, oblivious to the happy goings-on around her.

The two men parted with maudlin goodbyes and sincere promises of seeing each other in the morning for the trip to Port Royal. Mike wrapped Barbara in the towel on which she lay and carried her to their room.

Chapter 14

⚓

The lonely highway from Kingston to Port Royal was dark and unlit, showing only a pale ribbon in the moonlight. The highway had narrowed, and the orderly, yellow centerline had vanished miles back, giving the highway a gloomy feeling of desolation.

John Reid took a swig of his Red Stripe beer as he drove to the camp. The thought of burglary made him nervous, but it was necessary. The excavation had to be a failure so the harbor would be dredged, as he had told O'Reilly. In the beam from his headlights John saw what appeared to be two orange reflectors.

Must be that flea-bitten mutt Mike adopted, thought John. Just as he hated the man, he also hated anything connected with him. His mouth curled into a brutal sneer as he floored the accelerator, his fingers tapped the steering wheel to the tune he was humming. It was a rousing selection from Wagner called *The Ride of the Valkyries.* John clicked on his bright lights and drove from one shoulder of the road to the other, looking for the dog. The beam of the headlights zigzagged through the night, illuminating white winged insects before they splattered on the windshield.

The causeway extended into the sea for ten miles with only a sparse sprinkling of cactuses and mangroves on either side. He found the canine on a narrow strip where the vegetation thinned.

Like a loaded pistol, John aimed the smoking truck at the dog and stabbed the pedal. The frightened animal dashed onto the road, then went off it again; this made for a bumpy, neck-snapping ride, but John didn't care. He was having fun just trying to keep close.

The chase ended when John lost the animal in a thicket of mangroves. *Just as well,* he thought, *I need to tend to other things.* He lit a cigarette and drove back to the road.

John parked a quarter mile from camp and went the rest of the way on foot because he didn't want to be seen. He had the uneasy feeling of being watched and stopped walking several times to look around. John thought he saw the glowing eyes of the dog following him, but a second after he looked they would disappear. Curiously, they were red instead of orange. He was nearly at the camp so he quickened his pace. John's stomach tightened up a notch when he heard footsteps behind him. *Was it only his imagination? No, there it was again!* His heart pounding, he ran until the camp's mercury vapor lamp bathed him in its harsh, white light.

John sought the safety of the dive shack. The door was secured with a large padlock, but the hasp was cheap and ineffective. It came off with a twist of a screwdriver.

John peered over his shoulder. He couldn't see them, but he was sure the eyes were watching him, the intense red ones, not the fearful orange. He fell down as he entered the building. *Something grabbed my foot!* John's eyes were wide with terror, and his breath came in ragged gulps. Although he strained his ears to hear the ghostly steps that he knew were coming, the only sound he heard was his racing heart punctuated by his loud breathing.

He picked himself up from the wooden floor and switched on the flashlight. He felt foolish when he saw he had tripped over the threshold.

John opened the intake housings on the two water dredges and smashed the brass fins of the impeller with a hammer. Then he put the pieces in his pocket so they could not weld them back on. Mike would have to order new parts, and it might take a week to get them. By then John would have figured out a new way to slow the excavation. Now he needed to get rid of the more valuable artifacts. He found the table where Barbara kept the items discovered during the dig and played his light over it. The watch was in a small wooden box stuffed with rags. It sparkled like a rare jewel on display. When John reached for the watch, he heard the door creaking behind him, and switched off his flashlight. The dim light of the doorway framed a shadowy figure with two blazing eyes. They did not vanish as they had done earlier. Instead, they moved forward with slow, ponderous steps, followed by a rough grating of something dragging.

*　　*　　*

Paul had gone to bed early that night, but he did not get to sleep as planned. He tossed and turned endlessly. His mind focused on one thing: The watch was in danger, and that danger came from the road. When Paul got out of bed he wore a black shirt, nankeen breeches, gray silk stockings, and a soiled butcher's apron tied about his waist. Lying on the bed was the gleaming dagger he had found. His great hand wrapped around the handle perfectly, and he took several practice swings. The efficient blade swished through the air, dancing in the light. It seemed to hum happily now that they were together again.

With Paul's strange gait the quarter mile walk to the dive shack took nearly ten minutes. He found the threat in the shape of a small, nervous man who continually glanced about. The man walked so fast that he had disappeared, but Paul knew where he had gone. The road was a dead-end and had only one destination. It ended at Port Royal and death.

John was strangely calm as he stared into the seething eyes. He watched motionlessly as Paul came toward him, splitting the air with his silver dagger, and dragging the useless leg behind.

Swish. . .scrapppeee. . .swish. . .scrapppeee. . .swish. . .scrapppeee. . .

The ominous sound had a methodical cadence and helped to hypnotize John further.

Swish. . .scrapppeee. . .swish. . .scrapppeee. . .swish. . .scrapppeee. . .

The blade plunged deep into John's chest, shattering ribs and spattering blood everywhere. The live coals of Paul's eyes had a calming effect. John became tired and wanted to sleep. He smiled and closed his eyes and slept the uninterrupted sleep of the dead.

Paul picked up the watch and put it in his breast pocket. The weight felt reassuring against his chest. The watch was safe for now, but he needed to do one other thing to insure that safety.

He walked from the dive shack to the slack water of the harbor and found the rowboat of a fisherman. The boat was in need of repair, but it was seaworthy enough for the calm harbor. His stiff leg splashed into the water when he pushed off. Paul had to grasp it with both hands to pull it aboard.

Mark awoke shivering in the hospital room, and he drew the blankets tighter around him. Mark knew he was not alone. At the foot of the bed were two blazing red eyes. A figure emerged from the shadows with long dark hair and a beard. It chilled Mark to look at him. He was death. Mark was sure of that, and he knew he had come for him.

As if on cue, Paul shuffled alongside the bed and stared down at the frightened man. It was a pity Mark had to die, but he might tell the others about Paul's involvement in the accident. If anything should happen to Paul, who would look out for the watch? It had already been decided. Mark must die.

Paul slipped a huge hand over Mark's mouth, raised the dagger and completed his mission.

Chapter 15

⚓

Mike bolted upright in the darkness of the bedroom and let out a terrible scream. His skin glistened in the cold sweat of the nightmare; his eyes were wide with terror. Barbara jerked awake beside him.

"Oh, my God! Mike, are you all right?"

He whirled about and stared at Barbara for a moment, trying to decide if she was a part of the dream. When he was reasonably sure she wasn't he began to relax. "I am now."

"What happened?"

"I had a nightmare. I've been having the same one since we got here."

"You have?"

"Yes, it's about the excavation. Would you like to hear it?"

She nodded.

Mike sat up and made himself comfortable. "Well, Paul and I had scuba tanks and we dove the harbor. For some reason we found Port Royal was dry. Just like it must have been before the earthquake." He paused, allowing her time to question the statement he had just made. When she did not, he explained anyway. "There's a lot of symbolism here. Some of it may mean something. Some of it may not. Have you ever taken Psychology 104? Professor Phillips teaches it."

Barbara shook her head. "No, but I had an affair with him once."

"You didn't!"

Soft laughter.

"You're right. I didn't. But I could have, the old letch."

Mike crossed his legs and faced Barbara. "Well, in his class we analyzed dreams. It's speculated that most dreams have a very logical reason for occurring. Apparently, the excavation tripped it off."

"That would make sense."

"Well, as I said before Port Royal was dry and we had to pass through a large gelatinous bubble to reach it. After we had gone through it, we could breathe normally and no longer needed our scuba gear. We took it off magically with a wave of our hands and laid it neatly in a pile for our return. Then we walked down a narrow street until we came to a shop with a horrible sign hanging in front. Painted on the sign was a slaughtered pig strung up by his hind feet, while his snout dripped blood in a bucket."

"Oh, yuck!"

"Yeah, I agree. It was a butcher shop, I suppose. We entered and walked down a long, dark corridor. There were many intersecting passageways and we took a few of them. Suddenly, I was alone."

"Didn't Paul say anything before he left?" Barbara asked, wrapping the white sheet around her nakedness. The pink tip of her left breast peeked over the top, as if listening also.

"No, we didn't speak at all. We moved through the dream like we were in a trance. It was as if we had done this before and knew what to expect. Well, we had in previous dreams, but I never got beyond this point.

"Oh, this is first run?"

"Yeah, first run," Mike grinned. "So anyway, there I was alone. I remember I couldn't reach the end of the passage no matter how hard I'd try. The sides telescoped out before me. The air smelled so stale and musty, I wanted to choke. Probably the kind of air you'd expect to find in a tomb."

Barbara appeared to shiver from either the cold or the chilling story for she wrapped the sheet more tightly around her. Her eyes were bright, begging Mike to continue, which he did.

Mike told her about seeing a cross bathed in a pearlescent light at the end of the passage and he ran toward it. The closer he came, the more the cross took on an irregular shape. When he reached the end, the cross changed into an old, black man. He stood like a sentinel before Mike, blocking his path with upraised arms, resembling the same cross.

The man appeared as ancient as time itself. His thin, bony face was deeply lined with sun-wrinkles that radiated web-like from his potent, brown eyes and a troubled, thin slit of a mouth. He wore an old floppy straw hat, loose fitting gray trousers held up by a tightly knotted rope, and a red, yellow, and green-flowered Hawaiian shirt. The shirt hung limp like a sail waiting to catch the wind on a hot, lazy Caribbean afternoon. If that wind ever came, the dried out, old brown twig of a man would probably tumble along with it, wearing himself away to nothing, and leaving only the old straw hat and tattered clothing behind to show he had ever really existed at all.

"Stop! You must not go farther," the old man ordered, placing a skeletal hand on Mike's shoulder. It felt warm where he touched him. "Intense evil lurks beyond."

"Who are you?" Mike asked in a small, faraway voice.

"I am Captain Anthony, keeper of the light and protector of ships."

"Captain Anthony, I need to find my friend and get out of here. I saw the light and thought it might show the way."

The old man beamed proudly. "I provided the light to guide you and keep you away from the Dark One. You are in danger from his cold embrace everywhere. Everywhere except here, beside me."

"Will you walk with me while I search for my friend?"

"Yes, but are you sure you want to go beyond? It will be a bitter journey and full of risks."

Mike nodded.

"Very well, but I must warn you. You may not like what you find."

Captain Anthony took Mike's hand. "You must promise no matter what you see or hear you will stay by my side and not touch anything of your own free will. You must realize that there will be great fears and temptations trying to lure you away. Do not listen to them. They are only illusions and will not harm you if we do not stray from the chosen path."

Mike nodded and took the offered hand. As the old man turned, he saw that the light did not come from behind, as he had first thought, but emanated instead from the man's body. He glowed like a firefly, lighting their way.

The two entered a world of twisting, smoky shapes. They brushed Mike's skin leaving it intensely cold. It became freezing. The old man reached into his thin shirt and brought out a silver cross on a chain. He held the crucifix out front, like a flashlight guiding them into a strange, dark room. The light around them seemed to grow brighter, causing the icy blackness to recede. It illuminated the writhing, naked bodies of half a dozen enticing sirens. Their silky, waist-length hair twirled seductively around their lush bodies and they did wicked, provocative things with their flesh. The girlish creatures beckoned Mike to join them with waving, tapered hands and cold, blank eyes.

"Do not look at them!" Captain Anthony ordered.

The female demons kept their distance from the old man and concentrated on Mike. One slithered like a snake between his legs. He felt her groping hands on his most intimate places. Her touch was cold. He almost left Captain Anthony's side in his attempt to get away from her. The girlish demons saw this and gathered around, grabbing at Mike's clothes, until the old man whirled about and held the crucifix inches from them. They recoiled hissing, their bodies shriveling and turning a sickly yellowish green. Wriggling, twisting snakes oozed from their eyes and mouths and slithered to the ground creating a squirming, bilious-green sea. The serpents gazed at him with blazing eyes, their oily scales dripping with a thick slime.

"Keep walking!" Captain Anthony commanded. "They are only an illusion and will not harm you."

The two went on, stepping through the squirming, ankle deep mass, while the serpents hissed and slithered up their legs. Mike glanced to Captain Anthony and saw the reptiles were unable to cling to him. Try as they might, they would sizzle and fall away whenever they touched him, while Mike's feet were growing heavy with them. Five red-eyed snakes had slithered up both of his calves and were trying to climb further. He stamped his feet, trying to shake them free, but they hissed and coiled tighter.

A wall of fire ahead of them made Mike forget the snakes. The burning pyre seemed much more deadly because it held two human shapes in the center. The roaring orange-yellow flames danced and licked hungrily at the blackened skin, causing it to curl and peel off, popping and crackling as it went.

Mike peered into the flames at the blackening, putrid faces and saw that they resembled the old man and him. The sooty, parchment-like skin curled up to reveal their screaming skulls and glassy, horror-filled eyes.

When Mike stopped walking Captain Anthony gripped his hand more tightly than ever. "Don't be afraid! The Lord will protect you if you have faith in Him and do not venture from the chosen path. Come! Walk with me through the flames and I promise you, you will not be harmed."

There was no conscious movement on Mike's part. He seemed to float effortlessly forward and the two blackened scarecrows vanished. He looked at his legs and the snakes were gone, too.

They came to a chamber and Mike was startled to recognize his mother and father. His father was drunk, waving a gun. His mother was sitting on the side of the bed trying to calm him. Mike was stunned. When he looked to Captain Anthony, he found him grimmer than ever.

"These are my parents. I know they're dead, but maybe if I go to them now I can change things. You see, I wasn't there for them before."

"You can't help them. They are dead and nothing can change that. If you leave the path now the Dark One will be there to snatch you up."

Mike nodded gloomily.

His mother rushed over as they approached. Her tearful eyes were pleading. "Oh, Michael, thank goodness you're here! Your father's got a gun, and he's threatening to kill me. Please talk some sense into him before it's too late!"

Mike's eyes grew moist. He wanted to help her, but he had to remain firm. "Stay away from me! You're not my mother. She's dead."

"No, I'm not! Not if you hurry, Michael!"

"Leave me alone! You're not her! You're not even real."

She tugged at his hand. "Michael, please! He's coming for me. You must hurry!"

Mike heard heavy footsteps and turned. His father was coming and he wore a terrible scowl. He slapped his wife and grabbed her about the middle. Mike lurched forward to help her, and Captain Anthony gripped his hand more tightly and pulled him back. "No,

Mike! She's not your mother. She's part of the Dark One, an evil monster."

Mike watched his mother being dragged away, then turned to Captain Anthony and cried, "I know! I know she is, but everything is so real!"

"You wanted to come—so walk!"

Mike nodded and began walking again.

They were nearing the end of the chamber and saw a man standing before a butcher's block table with his back to them. As they got closer, the man turned and Mike saw that he was huge. He was so huge that he appeared to be growing out of his tight canvas shirt and brown breeches. He wore a soiled, blood red apron and hefted a gleaming dagger. The man had a bushy black beard and glittering red eyes, and he grinned when they approached. Mike could tell that this was the Dark One Captain Anthony had spoken of.

The monstrous apparition did not wait for them to come to him. He swung the dagger from side to side, as if he were cutting a terrible swath through some dense, invisible jungle. His gaze chilled Mike. He wanted to turn away and run, run like crazy, but the regular, pendulum movements made by the swishing blade hypnotized him. Suddenly it was not a dagger anymore, but a shiny gold pocket watch. The beautiful ship on its cover enthralled Mike. It swung rhythmically—back and forth—back and forth. The closer it got the deeper Mike's trance became. A hand slapped him hard. He turned and smiled at the old man.

"There he is! Look! Look and recognize the Dark One!"

Mike followed Captain Anthony's bony finger and was so shocked and terrified by what he saw that he woke up screaming.

The leering face had belonged to Paul, and the watch had become a menacing dagger again. It had been poised at the height of its vicious arc, ready to split him in two.

When Mike finished his story, he searched Barbara's face for a reaction. She raised her eyebrows in surprise. She let the sheet fall into a heap on her lap.

"Wow," she breathed, her mind racing, trying to think of all the implications.

Mike remained silent, letting the girl sort things out for herself.

"Do you think the dream has any truth in it?"

Mike laughed. "No, it's just a silly nightmare."

Barbara looked unconvinced. "I don't know. I have an aunt who swears she can tell the future from her dreams."

"Well, I'm not your aunt and this isn't one of her dreams."

"Just for the sake of argument though, let's say the dream might have a message. Look at the parallels. Hasn't Paul acted strangely since he found the watch? Even you said you get headaches from it."

"Okay, what are the other parallels?"

"I can't think of any right now," she admitted, "but that doesn't mean they don't exist."

"I think this is nothing more than a dream, and since we have to get up early let's try and get some sleep."

"I guess you're right."

Barbara lay down, but Mike could see she was still concerned. He turned off the light. She snuggled next to him, slipping an arm around his waist.

Mike laid awake the rest of the night thinking about the dream and wondering if any more parallels really did exist.

Chapter 16

Sunday, the fifth of July dawned overcast and rainy. The weather looked how Mike felt: gloomy and sick. From the hotel window he watched the rain slant from nothingness to the damp earth below. *Why did he drink all that beer?* Mike worked his tongue in the sandpaper of his mouth, tasting the sour beer and thinking of yesterday.

Barbara emerged from the bathroom fresh and vibrant in a peach halter and a pair of form-fitting tan slacks. Mike was astonished with what a woman could do when given a mirror and some makeup.

"Are you ready for breakfast?" she asked cheerily.

"I'm ready for anything that'll get this taste out of my mouth."

The Pelican Watch Restaurant was light and airy even though it was still raining outside. The second Barbara and Mike walked through the door a smiling hostess greeted them. She was a pretty, young girl who looked as though she was trying to grow up too fast. She wore gobs of eye shadow and lipstick and every part of her body seemed to wiggle when she walked.

They followed the girl single-file to a window booth. The parade began with three people, but ended with four. Kent was sitting at the counter with a cup of coffee when he saw them enter. He got up to follow and slipped into the seat opposite them. "Good morning!"

Mike grinned. "Hey, Kent! Somehow I didn't expect to see you here."

"I said I'd be."

"Yeah, I know, but we had a lot to drink last night."

"All the more reason I should be here. A promise made while drunk shouldn't be taken lightly."

A waitress appeared with a pad of paper to take their order. The men ordered ham and eggs, a cheese omelet, and two extra orders of bacon. Barbara had a warmed bran muffin with toast and a glass of orange juice.

Kent seemed amazingly fit and bright eyed. Mike suspected the coffee he was drinking had miraculous recuperative powers, so he ordered one, too.

When their breakfast came, everyone dug in except for Mike. Kent noticed his friend was not eating and lowered his fork. "Something troubling you?"

"I'm not very hungry," Mike said, pushing his plate away and taking a sip of coffee. "I didn't get much sleep last night. First the beer, then a really wild dream."

"Nightmare," Barbara corrected.

Kent waited to hear. When neither of them volunteered any more, he said, "Come on. You've got my interest. What was the nightmare about? The good queen Barbara being kidnapped by me, the evil man of the sea."

Mike laughed. "Nothing that simple."

"So tell me."

Mike did. When he mentioned Captain Anthony, Kent waved him silent. "When I'd go diving near Kingston, I'd see an old black man in a boat fishing. He was exactly as you described, the old straw hat, everything. I believe his name was Captain Anthony, and he lived in an old lighthouse that wasn't in use anymore. People said he'd been there as long as they could remember. When the government switched to automated lighthouses, they retired him also. I guess they let him live there because he had no place to go."

"Mike, there's another parallel," Barbara blurted.

"What's this about parallels?"

Mike smiled and waved a hand. "It's nothing. It seems that Barbara has set out to make this dream more than it really is."

"But, Mike, first Paul acting strangely, now the old man. Even his name is the same."

"I'll admit that there are certain similarities."

"Then if we find him," Barbara continued, "it'll prove the dream is true, and maybe he can tell us what is going on."

Kent raised his cup and took a drink of coffee. "Is there any more to the dream?"

Mike related the rest, including Paul's grisly part at the end.

"How well do you know Paul?"

"Fairly well, I guess. For two and a half, maybe three years," Mike said, his eyes questioning. "Why?"

"I'm just trying to get a handle on things. Is there any bitterness or jealousy between you?"

Mike shook his head. "No, but we did fight. I still haven't figured out the reason for it, though. I suppose he felt overworked and decided to take it out on me."

"Then he might be holding a grudge."

"He could be, but I doubt it. Do you think his part in the dream was a result of my still having some hostility toward him?"

"I don't know. Maybe."

All three were silent for a moment as a waitress in a pink rayon dress came by. She wasn't their server, but she warmed their coffees anyway and asked if everything was all right. They assured her everything was.

After sampling the coffee, Kent said, "Things do sound intriguing. If you want my help, what there is of it, you've got it for the next three days. I have to be back for the weekend diver trade," he explained. "Serious payments need to be made on that boat of mine."

"I appreciate the offer. We're extremely shorthanded, and any help we can get, no matter how temporary, is better than none."

Kent smiled and nodded while Barbara wondered if the dream really did contain a message.

After they had finished eating, they piled into Kent's van and were on the road by ten o'clock.

*   *   *

Tom Marino was the first to notice the door ajar on the dive shack. He waved the others back, crept over cautiously, and peered in.   What he saw would never leave him, and he would have nightmares about it.

A bloody body had been stripped naked, gutted, and hung from its heels like a side of beef. The remains did not look human because it lacked any head or arms. The police could not find them, but they discovered a gold tooth and ring at the bottom of a vat of nitric acid used to clean artifacts. The police fished them out with long plastic tongs, rinsed them off, and placed them in a plastic evidence bag. They also found a pile of bloody clothes containing a wallet that
indicated the forty-seven dollars, set of keys, cigarettes, matches, and sixteen two-inch pieces of triangular brass belonged to John Reid.

The two detectives assigned to the case were Greg Luckett and Bill Clayton. Greg was a big boned, black man, while Bill was just the opposite. He was a slender, white man who did not appear to be a policeman at all.

When the men had responded to the call a constable in front of the dive shack waved them over. The uniformed policeman motioned for them to look inside while he told them the details of the case. Bill looked away, while Greg gave the body a professional gaze. A rope had been tied around the corpse's ankles and then looped over a creaking ceiling joist. A million flies had invited themselves to the feast. The blood had become coagulated and dark, but an occasional drop still fell with clock-like regularity into a meandering puddle. Greg had a strange sense of *deja vu*, of seeing a mutilated body in the hospital that morning similar to this one.

The police questioned the three men who lived at the camp about whether they had heard or seen anything suspicious the night before.

When Paul's turn came he was in constant motion, scratching this, tugging that, folding and unfolding his arms and legs. He knew there might be trouble when he awoke that morning and found his hands and arms smeared with blood. At first, he was alarmed. He thought it might have been his. He took the bandages from his hands so he could examine them. The scrapes from his bout with the wall were healing nicely and there appeared to be too much blood for such minor wounds. Paul spat onto the floor to see if he might have coughed it up in his sleep. It appeared he hadn't because it was clear and frothy, the way spit should be. That's when Paul tore the blood-smeared sheets from his bed and buried them along with the bandages on the beach. He got a spade and dug a three-foot hole below the high water mark. Paul figured that when the tide came in it would smooth the sand over and hide any marks he had made.

Paul stared at the fresh bandages he had put on that morning and tried to answer the detective's questions.

"What did you do last night?" Inspector Luckett asked, leaning over his notepad on the table.

"I guess I went to bed around ten-thirty."

"You aren't sure?"

"Yes, it was ten-thirty."

"Did anyone see you?"

"Yeah, Tom and Nick did. We had a few beers in the dining room and talked."

"What did you talk about?"

"Oh, the usual things when guys get together. Girls, cars, and sports."

"Anything else?"

Paul shifted uneasily. "I don't remember. We talked about a lot of things."

"Was John Reid one of them?"

"No. Why should we talk about him?"

The detective flashed a cynical smile. "I don't know? You tell me."

"All I know is we didn't talk about him."

"Why all the bandages, Paul? Did you get into a fight?"

"Yeah, with a water dredge, but that happened yesterday morning."

"It did?"

"Yes."

The inspector glanced at his notes. "You said you went to bed around ten-thirty. Did anyone see you?"

"Yeah, I told you, Nick and Tom."

"Uh-uh. Did they actually see you go to bed or did they just see you leave the room?"

"They saw me leave the room."

"Where do you sleep?"

"In the dorm."

"What time did the others come in?"

"I'm not sure. I was asleep."

Paul was nervous. He wondered why the detective was asking him so many questions.

"I gather that John Reid is one of your associates. Do you know where he might be?"

"No, I don't. He goes home after work."

"What's your opinion of him?"

"He's all right, I suppose. I don't know him very well. Like I said before, he doesn't hang around after work."

"Who discovered the body?"

"You already know that."

"Yes, I do. But I want you to tell me."

"Tom did. All of us had noticed the door to the dive shack was open. However, he was the first to look inside."

"Did either of these men ever suggest that he was upset with John Reid? Maybe they had a falling out over something, a girl, perhaps."

"What do these questions have to do with John? Is that him in there?"

"We aren't certain, but we think it is."

Paul was shaken and took a moment to gather his thoughts. The headache began, and there was a new gleam in his eye. "My God, I didn't know that he would . . , "

"Who's he?"

"I'm sorry. I didn't mean to say anything."

"If you know something, Paul, then you'd better tell me."

"All right. His name is Mike Ryan, and he's our boss. He and Barbara Anderson went to Montego Bay for the weekend."

The detective began writing again. "Is she his girlfriend?"

"Yes, I think so. She cleans and preserves the artifacts that we find. Well anyway, they spend a lot of time together. John liked her, too. They left Friday morning in John's truck. I thought it a bit odd at the time, seeing how Mike dislikes the guy and all. He never did like the government putting John on the dive team." Paul watched the detective's pen with interest as it copied everything he said.

After the inspector was through questioning Paul, he left the dining hall and waited for his partner. Bill was interrogating Tom Marino in another room and later joined Greg in the car to compare notes.

"Have any luck?" Greg asked.

"Uh-uh. How about you?"

"Maybe. See what you make of this: Paul Kushe says a guy by the name of Mike Ryan runs things around here. He says that Ryan and John Reid didn't get along and that both men liked the same girl, a Barbara Anderson. He also said Ryan may have been the last one to see Reid alive."

"Sounds interesting. Do you think Kushe is telling the truth?"

"I don't know. It's easy enough to find out."

"Yeah."

"One thing bothers me, though. This killing and the one at the hospital have the same MO. They've got to be connected."

"Mark Sullivan worked here, so it's possible. Maybe one murder was used to cover the other," Bill suggested.

Greg considered. "Perhaps Reid knew something about the murder at the hospital, and the killer knocked him off to keep him quiet."

Bill mulled this over as he started the car and drove onto the highway. After several minutes, a reflection caught Greg's attention, and he told his partner to pull over. A rusting blue truck was concealed behind a thicket. Greg copied the license plate number while Bill looked inside and found a folded piece of paper on the faded dashboard. It contained a note on fancy city hall stationery that read:

> Pat O'Reilly
> Caribe Dredge and Dock
> 5223 Ocean View

He handed the paper to his partner. Greg checked the plate number with the radio dispatcher. When it came back registered to John Reid, he turned to Bill, holding the paper aloft. "Let's go! We got a lead."

*   *   *

Tom Marino spoke first. His voice was thin and quick, almost a whine, and his brown eyes jumped from Paul to Nick, and back again. "I don't care what people say! I didn't sign on this job to lock horns with any murderer." Tom scanned the others, searching for some reinforcement for what he was about to say. "I don't know about either of you, but as far as I'm concerned my work here is through. It was through the minute anyone got killed."

Paul and Nick nodded in agreement. They were seated at the dining table trying to decide their uncertain future. The terrible events of last night had made it necessary for them to rethink the entire situation.

Paul was worried that he might have committed those awful crimes. He liked the men who had been killed, and his thoughts confused him. If he was responsible, then why had he done it? He was also sorry for putting the police onto Mike's trail. He wasn't sure what had made him do that. Mike was one of the few people who had helped him and this was a cruel way to repay that kindness.

Fear was the prevailing emotion. No one left the sight of the others. When one of them would go outside, the other two would follow. If anyone went to the bathroom, he would have the others tagging along because they suddenly had the urge to go also. No one dared to take a nap for fear of being alone with the murderer. Instead, they talked until the others got back from Montego Bay. Each of them sought Mike's ear with their story, as if he was the favored parent and they were the attentions-seeking children.

Mike was shocked. How could this happen? His eyes sought out the others, and their blank faces seemed to mirror back the same inquiring look.

They discussed what to do over a supper of hot dogs, banana chips, and beer. Although everyone wanted to leave, they had to stay in Port Royal until the police investigation was completed. Mike thought it would help if he could get everyone thinking about something besides the murders. Archaeology had been the common bond that had brought them together, so it seemed the logical choice to reunite them now.

"I know this may sound a little strange under the circumstances," Mike began, "but I think we should continue with the excavation."

The whole group was surprised. Tom Marino seemed to speak for them all. "Mike, we've already discussed this, and we felt it's best if we leave as soon as we can. Until then we agreed to watch out for each other."

The others nodded and murmured agreement.

"All right, we will watch after one another," Mike said. "But if we continue with the excavation it'll take our minds off the murders and make the time go faster. I figure since we can't go anywhere anything that'll help the time go by is certainly worthwhile."

Paul's voice boomed angrily. "But we can't continue with the excavation because someone broke the dredges."

"Can they be fixed?"

"I know a place where we could probably borrow some," Kent suggested. "They're used commercially and may be too large for what you have in mind, but I'm sure we can adapt them to what we need."

"We'll see to it first thing in the morning," Mike said, smiling confidently. "Is there anything else?"

"Yeah. I don't want to rain on your parade," Tom Marino said, "but we still have a killer running around loose. What do you propose we do about that?"

"We should stay in groups of two or three."

"What about me?" Barbara asked. "In case you've forgotten, I'm a woman. I need to be alone for certain things."

"When you have to go to the bathroom one of us will accompany you."

"One of us may be the killer!" Tom cried.

The room fell silent while everyone considered the truthfulness of his statement. Although they didn't mean to, it was hard to keep their nervous eyes from drifting around the room at the others.

Barbara shattered the silence when she said, "Thanks, Tom, for reminding me that I'm in great danger every time I go to the bathroom."

Her comment took the edge off the group's mood, and there were several nervous chuckles.

"Now that we have this noisy mob under control," she said, "I'll reveal my choice for guardian. I trust Mike."

"Thank you for your confidence," Mike said, and turned to Kent. "You don't have to be involved in this. The murders make this a new ball game, and all previous agreements are off."

"I'm here," Kent said, smiling with boyish ease, "and I'd still like to help."

Mike nodded thanks and faced the others. "Since there are six of us I think we should divide into threes. If the killer is among us, then he'll be outnumbered two to one. Maybe that will make him think before anyone else is hurt. I propose Kent, Tom, and Nick should be in one group and Paul, Barbara, and I in the other."

Kent appeared surprised, and Mike explained. "Since we were together for the weekend, I thought it best if we split up."

Kent nodded.

"Does anyone have any questions?"

"Yes, I have one," Barbara said. "Are we leaving when the police say we can? No matter what we find in the harbor?"

"Yes, when they say it's safe and you're free to go."

"What'll we do until we get the new dredges?" Nick asked.

"Well, we'll help Barbara clean artifacts or . . . paint the buildings. See, there's a lot to do if you only stop to think about it. Are there any more questions?"

No one said anything.

"Okay, then I suggest we start working together again."

*   *   *

A revolving light glimmered atop the lighthouse in the distance as Barbara, Mike, Kent and King walked across the dunes. The sun was low in the sky and its golden splendor melted away the harsh edges of their shadows.

Mike told Kent about the boat they had gotten from Key West a few weeks before. It was a new, thirty-six-foot Bertram with side-scan sonar and a custom depth recorder. The person operating the recorder punched in the depth he wanted, plus an event alarm. If the depth changed suddenly a buoy was automatically dropped to mark the spot while the recorder sounded a shrill five-second blast.

Kent told Barbara and Mike that it was rumored that Henry Morgan, the famous pirate, buried twelve chests of gold in these dunes. Kent said that when he was a kid, he would roam the area with a small shovel and dig at anything that looked the least bit suspicious. He had been digging one day near the lighthouse and had found a bony arm, and gave the building a wide berth ever since.

When they came closer to the lighthouse, the old black man from Mike's dream opened the door and smiled at them. Mike stared in total shock. He had suspected the man might be there, but never thought he would be exactly as he had appeared in the dream. King wagged his tail excitedly and bolted toward the old man. Captain Anthony knelt to greet the dog, then stood when the three approached, extending his hand. "Hello, Mike. I'm Captain Anthony. I knew you'd come. God's will is strong."

Mike shook his hand, and said, "These are my friends, Barbara and Kent."

"I know you must have a lot of questions," Captain Anthony said. "Why don't you come inside, and I'll try to answer them."

The three went into the building and looked around. Since hurricane Gilbert destroyed the lighthouse keeper's house in 1988, the old man's whole world was crammed into a forty-foot in diameter circular room. Along the walls were a large old-fashioned writing desk, a bed with a green blanket, a cast-iron wood stove, and some kitchen cabinets with glass doors. In the center was a rectangular table with six wooden chairs. Everyone sat while Captain Anthony put on a pot of tea.

"How do you know who I am, and why have you been in my dreams?" Mike asked.

Captain Anthony set the teapot on the nearest burner and looked up. "Because you've been in mine. Does that surprise you?"

"Yes, it does."

"Let me explain." Captain Anthony pulled out a chair and sat. "I suppose I should start at the beginning. Six months ago I had a dream about a man named Matthew Hudson. He lived in Port Royal before the earthquake in 1692. I didn't think much of it until I began having the same dream every night. I wondered why I was having these dreams. I found a book in the library about the city's history and was surprised to find the man mentioned. It explained that he was involved in witchcraft and several murders. It also said that he died in the great earthquake. Later, I had dreams about you and the excavation."

"We found a pocket watch with the name Hudsen engraved inside the cover, but we were unsure of whether it belonged to a man named Hudsen with an 'e' or Hudson with an 'o'," Mike said.

"Yes, I know. His name is spelled with an 'o' and that watch is cursed, and it must be destroyed."

"I can't do that," Barbara said. "It belongs to the Jamaican Government. Besides, we don't know where it is."

The old man appeared concerned. "You lost it?"

"Yes, it was stolen last night," Mike said.

Captain Anthony's bony face looked more worried than ever. "That makes things very difficult."

"What do you mean?"

"Do you believe in black magic, Mike?"

"I don't know? I've never thought about it."

"Well, it's real and it's very powerful. Matthew Hudson is a henchman of the devil. That's where he gets his power. When the earthquake came and he saw he was going to die, he transferred his soul to that watch you found. He drowned and the watch was safely entombed in the sea for three hundred years. However, true evil never dies, you know. You disturbed his tomb when you unearthed the wicked city and found his watch. Now he is free again."

"Shouldn't we tell the police?" Barbara asked.

"I'm afraid they wouldn't believe you. Since Hudson died three hundred years ago, he doesn't have a physical body that you can arrest. What we're dealing with now is his spirit. He could take many forms, living or dead—human or animal—male or female. The Dark One chooses whatever suits his purpose at the moment."

"Who is this dark one?"

"That is what I call Matthew Hudson because his soul is as dark as the black clothes he wears."

"I'm terribly sorry if we caused this to happen," Mike said.

"You can't be blamed for something you weren't aware of. But it's up to you to stop him before he can rally his army and become too powerful."

"What's this about an army?"

"The Dark One has many in his army of evil. The Adolph Hitlers and Charles Mansons are everywhere, even on this very island, waiting for the right leader. It won't be easy getting rid of him, but there are eight of us now."

"Eight?"

"Yes. You and your friends make six. With Prince and me there are eight."

"Prince?"

"Yes, my dog," Captain Anthony said, and looked down at Prince. The retriever wagged his tail happily and licked the old man's hand.

"King's yours?" Barbara asked.

"Yes. I sent him to watch over you."

"I'm glad you did. Have you heard about the murders?"

"No. What happened?"

Barbara related the grisly details. The old man shook his head. "It's begun."

"What should we do?" Mike asked.

"Why don't you stay here? The lighthouse has a strong door, and the walls are six feet of solid stone."

"That's a terrific idea, but do you have enough room for six people?"

"Yes, I have plenty. I keep some cots in a shed outside for emergencies."

"Super! We'll tell the others we're moving and get our belongings."

The old man reached into his pocket and retrieved a small bottle attached to a stout leather thong. "Mike, before you go would you wear this?"

Mike saw Captain Anthony was holding something. "What's that?"

"This bottle contains holy water and a gold cross. A priest has blessed it. I tied a leather strap to it so you could wear it around your neck to always keep it close to you."

"Thank you. I appreciate the thought, but I don't believe I'll need that."

Captain Anthony appeared disappointed, so Barbara took the bottle of holy water from his hand. She turned to Mike and hung it around his neck, kissing his cheek and whispering to him, "Please do this for me!"

Barbara held Mike's hand and said to Captain Anthony, "Mike will be happy to wear this because he knows how much his safety means to me."

"Excellent!"

When they were back at camp and told the others what had happened at the lighthouse, everyone expressed disbelief.

"I don't believe you're listening to what some old geezer said about evil spirits being inside that watch," Paul said. "Granted our troubles began about the same time as the discovery, but an evil watch? You surely don't expect us to believe that?"

"No, I don't," Mike said. "Nevertheless, I think you should trust me enough to listen to what I have to say."

"All right then, go ahead."

"I had a dream about this old man and the watch. When I mentioned this to Kent, he said the man lived in a lighthouse in Kingston. I went to visit him tonight, and he was exactly like I had seen him in the dream."

"Maybe it was just a coincidence."

"No. I don't think so. He said he was having similar dreams. He told me they included a man named Matthew Hudson. He did some research. One book said this man was a witch and that he was involved in some murders. That name is also engraved in the watch we found."

"Well, I don't believe in ghosts," Paul said. "However, you're the boss. If you want to move into a lighthouse and go chasing after evil spirits, then you go right ahead."

"What about you guys?" Mike asked.

Tom shook his head in disbelief. "This expedition's getting crazier by the minute, but I guess I'll go along with everyone else."

Nick agreed with Tom.

"I was hoping for a little more enthusiasm," Mike said, "but I guess I'll have to take what I can get. Let's get ready to move."

Barbara packed the food and dishes into large boxes while the men gathered clothing and sleeping bags. Since it was dark outside, she went to the dive shack to get a flashlight.

Barbara found two flashlights on the shelf by the compressor. Picking them up, she noticed one was much lighter than the other was. Curious, she turned the black plastic rim and opened it. Instead of batteries a blood stained white cloth was packed inside. The police had not found John Reid's arms or head. She had visions of the cloth containing a bloody finger or an ear. The grisly thought nearly made her drop the light and flee from the room, but she could not let herself do that. She was determined to hold her ground because she figured the men would love to see the only girl on this excavation act like a frightened woman. She bolstered her courage and forced herself to look again. What was the cloth doing there, and what did it contain? Barbara pulled it from the case with two shaky fingers. The cloth opened revealing the thin frayed edges of a torn bed sheet. She tugged at the corners, careful to avoid the bloodstains. The gold pocket watch fell onto the table. Barbara heard footsteps and turned to see who it was.

"Look! I've found the watch," she exclaimed. Paul stood in the doorway, and the terrible look on his face chilled her to the bone. Barbara could tell that this was not the man she knew.

"Give me the watch, Rose Marie." The body before her belonged to Paul, but not the deep voice.

Barbara hid the watch in her hand with the finesse of a magician and took several steps backward. "Who's Rose Marie? You know my name is Barbara."

Paul moved forward. "No, it's Rose Marie. You had me fooled at first, but not anymore. I know you're a witch. You escaped from my shop and made the earth heave up in anger. Now, through your witchcraft, you've made the watch disappear. But you won't escape me this time. I've come to claim what's mine and put you in your grave forever."

"I told you! I'm not your damned Rose Marie, and I don't have the watch."

He laughed, but it was not gay or humorous at all. "Oh, how well I know you! You're trying to trick me again."

If he wanted to believe she was Rose Marie, then so be it. Barbara pointed a determined finger at him. "If you take another step, I swear, I'll start another earthquake!"

He hesitated, unsure.

"I mean it! Don't come any closer!" she warned, glaring at him.

"You're trying to trick me," he said, moving forward as if testing her, still unsure if he was doing the right thing. "But I am the one to be feared. I'm already dead, so you can't hurt me as you did before. I have magic, too. Strong magic."

"Yes, I can still hurt you! My magic is more powerful than yours," Barbara said. She glanced at the vats of nitric acid they used to clean the artifacts. "I can destroy your precious watch. Here, if you still want this, then you'll have to get it." She tossed the watch hoping it would land in the tank. It did and made a reassuring plop.

Paul rushed over to the vat and peered in. The acid was clear, and he saw the watch lying on the bottom. He looked at her, grinning. "Your magic didn't work! There's only two-feet of water in here."

He thrust both hands deep into the tank, groping for the watch. Paul roared in agony as the acid seethed and bubbled. When he withdrew his arms, the skin and muscles of his hands and forearms were melting off in long smoking strips. His reddish tissue had the consistency of overcooked meat. It fell away from his bone, and the watch fell to the floor. As he bent to pick it up Barbara saw her chance. She grabbed a plastic bucket from the floor and scooped it full of acid.

Paul was on his knees, trying to pick up the watch with his smoking hands, when Barbara splashed him. He howled as the voracious liquid gurgled about his head and shoulders. She scooped the bucket full again and threw it in his face. Terrible screams rocked the building. He clawed at his eyes, tearing away huge chunks of bubbling flesh.

"You made the water boil with your magic!" Paul yelled.

The smoking pits of his eyes were fiery craters, and most of his nose was gone. When he tried to make a fist, he found his arm was only a smoldering stump. All of his fingers lay in the seething puddle on the floor.

Barbara heard voices outside and ran through the doorway into Mike's arms.

"Thank God you're all right!" Mike said relieved. "I was so worried I—"

She burst into tears and cut him off. "Paul—the watch—in there!"

Without looking behind him, Mike passed her to the person in behind him. Kent appeared confused to have a sobbing girl thrust into his arms. He opened his mouth to protest, but Mike had already gone inside.

The interior of the dive shack resembled a ghastly scene from a horror movie. A body oozed and bubbled ominously as it lay on the floor in a pool of disgusting fluid. Large portions of its arms and torso were stripped of skin and muscle, exposing gleaming white bone. A distorted hand looked as if it had tried to clutch the glittering watch.

As Mike reached for the watch, Paul popped up like some grotesque windup toy. His head resembled a melting pink and white candle with the wax running down. He had no eyes, nose, or lips, and the slit of his mouth was oddly grinning.

Paul lunged forward, hitting Mike in the chest and bowling him over. Mike was trapped beneath him in a pool of acid, while a forearm that smelled of rotten eggs was driving his throat into the floor. Everything his slimy skin touched burned.

Kent stormed in and grabbed Paul by the shoulders. His fingers sank deep into the warm flesh until they hit bone, then the huge body bent, releasing its prey.

Still clutching the watch, Mike skirted the smoking ball of meat and hurried to the ocean. His body ached as if a thousand angry bees were attacking it. Plunging into the water, Mike rinsed the foul liquid from his skin. When Mike was through, he joined the others outside the dive shack.

"It seems Paul thought I was some girl named Rose Marie," Barbara explained. "According to him she was a witch, and his death was all her fault. He said he wanted his watch, and he was going to kill me. I was never so scared in all my life!"

Mike moved beside her and placed a comforting hand on her shoulder. "That's all over. You needn't worry about it anymore."

Barbara nodded and smiled.

*   *   *

When they returned to the lighthouse and Barbara told Captain Anthony what had happened, he said, "Remember what I told you? About the Dark One not having a material body?"

"Yes."

"Well, until we destroy that cursed watch, he is free to choose another. This time it might be any one of us." Captain Anthony looked about gravely. "I suppose the Dark One chose Paul because he was best equipped to serve his needs at the time. There's no denying Paul was big and strong, perhaps easily swayed."

"Surely you're not suggesting we have anything to fear from any one of us?" Barbara asked.

"Yes, I am."

"No! I won't accept that. Paul is dead, and we're through with this horrible mess."

Captain Anthony looked at Barbara. "I'm afraid we won't be through as long as that watch is around."

"Then throw it in the ocean!"

"No," Mike said. "Captain Anthony's right. We've got to see this thing through to the end."

Barbara looked at him as if he were crazy. "I don't believe you people! Do you realize you're giving him another chance to kill us all?"

"No, Barbara, I'm doing what has to be done. Unless this watch is destroyed he'll return."

"Where did you put the watch?" she demanded.

Mike refused to tell her.

Barbara glared at him and thrust her hand out. "Give me the watch, and I'll end it right now!"

"No, Barbara, listen. I have a plan."

"So have I. Give me the watch."

"Please listen to me. Okay?"

She did, and Mike explained his plan.

Chapter 17

Mike and the others were walking to the boat when the detectives assigned to the murder investigation pulled up in their car. The two men got out and approached the group.

"Mr. Ryan?" Inspector Luckett asked.

"Yes?" Mike wondered who these men were.

"I'm Inspector Luckett, and this is my partner, Inspector Clayton. We'd like to ask you a few questions."

"We're in a hurry, Inspector. Can this wait until I return?"

"No. It can't."

"We'll only be gone an hour."

"Mr. Ryan, this is a murder investigation and you're our prime suspect. If you go out in that boat, you could flee the country. I can't let that happen."

Mike was desperate; he needed to dispose of the watch before anyone else died. The weather was already hot and humid, so the inspector shed his suit coat. Mike could see the blue-steel, thirty-eight automatic on the policeman's hip. Wanting to distract him Mike craned his neck and stared past the two detectives. "I don't believe it! There goes a naked woman."

When Inspector Luckett turned to look, Mike snatched the gun.

The detective spun around and found himself facing his own gun. "You're making things tough on yourself, Ryan. Give yourself up. This won't do you any good."

Mike shook his head and held up the watch. "Not until I dispose of this. Inspector Clayton, give your gun to Captain Anthony."

The policeman frowned, but did as he was told. "You're only making things worse, Ryan. Drop your gun before it's too late."

"Mike, you're making a terrible mistake," Barbara said. "Just explain to them what it is that you want to do."

"Have you forgotten that there's another dead body in the dive shack? And have you forgotten who splashed him with acid?"

Barbara reassessed the situation. "Perhaps you're right. Let's get rid of that damned watch."

"What's this about another body?" Inspector Luckett demanded.

Mike stepped to the side and waved the gun at the policemen. "I'll tell you about it later. Let's get on the boat."

"You realize this is kidnapping," the detective said.

"Yes, but once I get rid of this watch I'll return your gun. You can do anything you want then."

They went aboard the boat. A half mile from shore, Mike ordered Captain Anthony to help tie everyone up and have them sit around the deck. After he had finished, Mike tied the old man's hands, too. Then he went to the GPS and the depth recorder, programmed the equipment, and went to the buoy rack near the stern. He locked Prince in the cabin, then took the policeman's handcuffs and handcuff key, slipped the key into his back pocket and handcuffed his own hands behind his back.

Mike lowered himself to the deck and explained. "All we do now is wait. The boat is self-sufficient. I've set the course on the GPS to pass over the blue hole, and I set the depth recorder to launch a buoy when we reach sixty feet and another at two hundred feet of water. I've tied an Emergency Positioning Radio Beacon to the first buoy, so it will send out a signal for us to be rescued. The reason I chose sixty feet is because the water doesn't get that deep until we get near the blue hole. I've replaced the second buoy with the watch so it will sink in deep water. Barbara gave me the idea, and I expanded on it."

"Why didn't we just destroy the watch?" Tom asked.

"We couldn't do that because gold is indestructible. Besides, even if we did manage to destroy it, what's to stop Matthew Hudson from finding a new home?"

"Why did you tie everyone up?" Nick asked.

"It's a precaution in case Matthew Hudson invades anyone's body. This way he can't possibly get loose."

"What's this about?" Inspector Luckett demanded.

Mike explained the events of the last few days and how Matthew Hudson and the watch figured in.

The detective frowned. "This story sounds like a lot of hogwash to me. You're just trying to create an alibi for yourself."

"If you don't believe me, then maybe you'll believe Captain Anthony."

"Everything Mike has told you is true," the old man said.

"I'm supposed to believe you? You're probably involved in the murders with him," the detective said. He suddenly shivered as Matthew Hudson tried to invade his body, thrashing about and struggling with the handcuffs.

Tom burst into motion, and the policeman became still. He threw his body about, wildly kicking, and jerking until he rolled on the deck.

Mike said, "Everyone is tied up, Matthew. Since there's no way for you to get free why don't you leave?"

Kent began to convulse as Matthew Hudson's soul invaded his body. He thrashed about violently, bumping into Captain Anthony.

"Matthew, for God sake leave us alone!"

Captain Anthony crashed into the scuba tanks. A bright trickle of blood ran down his right ear.

Kent stopped struggling and glared at Mike. "Give me Rose Marie and the watch, or the old man dies!" he boomed.

Mike needed to stall him for about fifteen minutes, until the boat had time to reach the blue hole. "I don't know who Rose Marie is, and I don't have the watch anymore. I turned it over to the police."

The alarm sounded on the depth recorder and the EPRB shot from the stern.

"What's that?" asked Matthew.

"Oh, it's nothing, just a buoy going in the water."

Matthew clutched Captain Anthony with his feet. "Give me the woman and the watch, or the old man dies," he repeated.

"I told you. I can't."

Matthew rammed the old man's face with his broad forehead, and he grinned at Mike, his face shiny with blood.

"Please stop!" Barbara shouted.

"Not until I get what I want."

Matthew lunged at Captain Anthony again. There was a sickening crack, followed by a moan from the old man. "Give me the woman and the watch."

Mike guessed he needed ten more minutes until they reached the blue hole.

"Give them to me!" Matthew shouted.

Captain Anthony struggled against his powerful legs. "Don't you do it, Mike!"

Matthew flung himself forward again. The old man slammed onto the deck and was quiet.

The rumble of another boat broke the silence. Mike looked over the gunnel and saw it had the red and white bow of a government patrol boat.

"Ahoy there!" an officer bellowed through a loudhailer from the Jamaican Coastal Defense Craft. "Are you in need of assistance?"

Mike cursed silently. He had not expected the EPRB would bring help so soon. "No!" he yelled, rising up a bit. "Everything's fine! We were taking on some water earlier and our bilge pump wouldn't work, but we fixed it! Thanks anyway!"

The officer nodded, scanning their boat with a suspicious eye. Two other men joined him. One of them pointed and made several sweeping gestures with his hand while they talked. A fourth man came out from the cabin carrying some automatic weapons and began passing them out. Drug smuggling and hijacking were rampant in the Caribbean, and this boat looked very suspicious.

The officer announced, "We have received a distress call from your vessel, and we need to check it out! I order you to heave to immediately! We are coming aboard!"

The Bertram did not stop and the officer shouted, "Heave to immediately! That's an order from the Jamaican Government!"

Still the boat did not slow, and the government patrol boat closed the gap between them. A man in a blue uniform leaped aboard carrying an automatic rifle. He scurried forward, training his weapon in a deadly arc on the people seated around him. Another man hopped aboard, throttled the engines down and took the boat out of gear.

Mike squirmed frantically. "Don't do that! We have to stay moving!"

The officer leaped aboard. "What's going on here?" he demanded. His uniform was freshly starched, and he wore black high-topped boots.

Mike made up a story. "You must get this boat away from here immediately! We found an old floating mine in this area, and I've set a small explosive charge to detonate it. It'll blow up in less than five minutes."

Inspector Clayton trembled as Matthew Hudson invaded his body. "Don't listen to a word he says! He's a liar and a thief. I'm a Kingston Constable, and I was trying to stop a hijacking of this boat when they pulled a gun and handcuffed me. You'll find my identification in my left hip pocket."

The people seated around the deck erupted in a frenzied chorus of "Don't listen to him!" and "He's a liar!"

The officer shook his head. "Everyone shut up! Seaman Johnson," he yelled to the man nearest the controls, "Get us the hell away from here. And be quick about it."

Johnson nodded and jammed the boat into gear. The officer motioned to the remaining seaman on the patrol boat, indicating they should follow them.

"Seaman Thorez, see that everyone's tied up. Starting with the gentleman who claims that there's a mine in the water."

As the officer bent to retrieve Inspector Clayton's identification, Mike took the handcuff key from his back pocket and quietly began fumbling with his handcuffs.

Inspector Luckett shouted, "I'm the only police officer here! I say that that man who says he's a constable is the real phony."

"We'll find out who's telling the truth," the officer said, flipping open the policeman's ID case. He looked at the photo on the identification card. "I'm sorry, Inspector Clayton, but I can't untie you until I know more."

Inspector Luckett spoke up. "I have credentials, too."

The officer found his wallet, glanced at it and placed it along with the other man's ID. He eyed the group seated around him and asked, "Why is everyone tied up?"

An explosive burst of machine gun fire hit the officer and the seaman at the helm, cutting them in two. The officer fell on Greg while the seaman slammed into the door of the cabin and slid to the deck, smearing a wide trail of blood. His eyes were open as if staring in shock at his own juices. The man on the patrol boat made a dash for the radio, but Seaman Thorez shot him down before he had taken three steps.

When the firing ceased, the Seaman Thorez came over to Mike and raised his rifle barrel to his left temple. "I told you I'd find a way," he uttered in Matthew Hudson's terrible voice. "Perhaps now you'll tell me what I want to know."

Barbara was not prepared to see Mike's head splattered all over the boat. "The watch is in the buoy rack—near the transom," she blurted.

Matthew looked at her curiously. "You're Rose Marie!"

"Yes, I am. I've been trapped inside the watch just like you. Now I've come to pay you back for what you did to me," Barbara heard herself say in a strange voice.

"How? You're tied up. I'll deal with you after I get the watch."

Captain Anthony had not tied her very tightly because he was afraid of hurting her. While Matthew trudged to the rear of the boat, Rose Marie wriggled out of her ropes and ran to the controls. She jerked the throttles wide-open, causing the deck to heave so violently that the motion almost threw Matthew into the water. He caught himself and threw his body to the deck. The watch flew from his hand and skittered to a stop a few feet from Rose Marie.

She scooped it up and ran for the cabin.

Matthew howled in surprise and caught her when she tried to open the door.

Rose Marie screamed and tried to run away, but her feet slipped on the gore-spattered deck. She slammed her head back into his.

Matthew's nose exploded in a blinding flash of pain. His grip loosened, and she tried to open the door again. It opened several inches and stopped, Prince growling in the crack. The dead seaman lay in a heap at the foot of the door, jamming it.

Rose Marie tried kicking him away. She felt the powerful arms tighten around her again. Kicking and screaming, she fought the steely fingers that were trying to pry her hands apart and get the watch.

Suddenly she heard a commotion, and the hands were gone.

Even though they were still tied all the others jumped to their feet and rushed Matthew, butting him with their heads or kicking him. Mike's hands were free and he struck Matthew on the head with a diving weight until the man crumpled to the deck.

Barbara rushed to Mike and he gathered her into his arms. "Oh, Mike, I was so scared. Thank heavens you were able to knock Matthew out.'

"Everything's fine for now, but we still have to get rid of that watch."

Reaching out with trembling hands, Barbara handed the watch to Mike. "Here, you take this! I don't want to be responsible for it any longer.

Mike took the watch from her and began to shudder as Matthew tried to invade his body.

"Matthew, stop it! I'll never let you have this! Never!"

All at once, Mike stopped struggling and seemed at ease. Matthew laughed in his deep voice. "See, Rose Marie! I told you I would get the watch back."

Barbara went from the height of triumph to the valley of despair in an instant. "Oh no! This can't be happening!"

Mike began shuddering again and fell to the deck, convulsing. His body twisted and turned like it was fighting with itself. Mike shouted, "I'll never let you have the watch! You'll have to kill me first."

Mike stopped struggling and stood up. He looked at Barbara with sorrowful eyes. "Barbara, I don't want to do this, but it's the only way."

Barbara drew closer. "Mike, what are you talking about?"

Mike motioned for her to stop. "Barbara, keep away! I can't be trusted any longer! Matthew is becoming too strong."

Mike's face contorted in pain. He grabbed a diving weight in one hand and held the watch in the other.

"Barbara, no matter what happens, always remember that I love you."

Barbara was in tears. "Mike, why are you telling me this? What are you going to do?"

"Matthew is gaining control of my body. I need to do something now to make sure he doesn't ever get free to kill again. Believe me, this is for the best."

The shrill three-second blast of the depth recorder signaled the boat was in two hundred feet of water.

"Goodbye, Barbara!" Mike said, giving her a brief smile. Mike took three deep breaths, holding the third.

"No Mike!" She took a step toward him.

He flung himself into the water and headed for the bottom of the blue hole.

Barbara ran to the railing. "Mike! Mike, come back to me!"

She began climbing the railing when she felt Captain Anthony's hands pull her back.

"Let him go, Barbara. Mike has decided to battle this demon on his own terms. Come. We need to pray for his safety."

Captain Anthony and Barbara untied the remaining crewmembers, gathered everyone in a circle on the rear deck and had them hold hands.

Captain Anthony bowed his head, "Heavenly Father, who gives us victory over evil through the shed blood of your Son, we thank you for your wisdom and protection. As Mike battles this evil force, shield him with your armor. Give him the strength to prevail that only you can provide. We put our faith and trust in you and in your perfect will. We pray for these things in Jesus holy and precious name. Amen!"

Everyone automatically went to the railing to search for Mike. They stayed at their vigil for over an hour, hoping to see some sign of their friend. Unfortunately that never happened. A storm came up and began pelting them with rain. The wind and seas were mounting and everyone but Barbara agreed to go back to shore.

"We can't leave him! Mike wouldn't do that if it was anyone of us in the water!"

"Barbara, we've done all we can. No one could have survived underwater that long," Kent said, moving to calm her.

"Stay away from me! If you were a true friend you wouldn't let this happen."

Captain Anthony had been keeping an eye on the gathering clouds. "Kent's right, Barbara. We must think of our own safety. There's a storm coming and the ocean will get rough."

Inspector Clayton was feeling a little sick and welcomed a chance to head back to land. "Kent, you're a licensed sea captain. Why don't you pilot the boat back to shore?"

Barbara looked at the others in shock. "I don't believe you people! How can you do this?"

Trying to reason with her Kent said, "Barbara, we all agreed it's useless to stay here any longer. If Mike was still alive we would have seen him by now."

Even though the others had made up their minds Barbara refused to abandon him. "All right. You go in, but before you leave put me on the Jamaican Defense boat. I'm staying here to wait for Mike."

"We can't do that. We have to tow that boat back into shore and turn it over to the authorities."

Barbara glared at the others, tears streaming down her cheeks. "Fine! You do what you need to do. I just hope you people can live with yourselves knowing that you abandoned a friend when he needed you!"

Turning in a huff, Barbara went to the port railing and stared out to sea.

Captain Anthony came alongside her and said, "I'll help you look for him."

Barbara gave him a weak smile and brushed away a tear. "Thanks! I think you're the only friend I have left in the world."

*   *   *

When the detectives submitted their report of the incident they said nothing of the evil spirit. They knew their superiors would never believe them. The inspectors explained they were trying to arrest the killer when he hijacked the camp's boat. The detectives had followed in a small motor boat, spotted a Jamaican Coastal Defense Craft and flagged it down. When they had gone aboard and informed the soldiers of the situation, a chase and gun battle resulted. Three members of the patrol boat, Mike Ryan and the murderer were killed.

*   *   *

Everyone dreaded making plans for Mike's memorial service in the days ahead. However, no one was more depressed than Barbara was. She could not eat and slept very little. One particularly sad morning she decided to go on the beach for a walk. She found a dry spot on the sand and sat facing a beautiful sunrise. The sea and distant clouds were touched with dazzling purple and the sun was just starting to peek out from behind a golden cloud. Brilliant rays of light emanated above that cloud and glistened on the tears streaming down Barbara's cheeks.

"God, I have always tried to do what's right and please you. But lately I've begun to question my faith. Do you really love me as it says in the Bible? If you truly do, why have you brought Mike into my life and then snatched him away from me? What good can come of this?"

Closing her eyes, Barbara dabbed at her tears with a hanky. When she opened them she saw someone was standing in front of her, blocking the light.

"A penny for your thoughts," Mike said, holding out a coin.

"Mike? Is that you?"

Mike pulled Barbara up from the sand and gave her a big hug. "Yes, it's me!"

She turned up to him with tears in her eyes. Kissing each one away, he moved lower toward her lips. When their lips finally met the kiss was like nothing they had ever experienced before. Passion guided this simple act but the kiss said so much more. It told of love lost, then found again. Lastly, it spoke of two souls becoming one.

When the kiss broke Barbara said, "We thought you were dead. How did you manage to escape?"

"It's a long story. Why don't we start at the beginning?"

"All right." Barbara said, holding his hand because she didn't want to lose him again.

"Well, when we were on the boat Matthew had me worried. He was gaining control of me and I was becoming weaker. I knew had to do something to prevent that from happening."

"But why did you choose to jump in the water with the watch? Couldn't you have just tossed it over board?"

"No. At that point Matthew was inside of me, not the watch. I had to get the watch and Matthew away from everyone else. Then I somehow had to convince Matthew to leave my body and enter the watch again."

"How did you do that?"

"Believe it or not, Captain Anthony supplied the answer."

"He did?"

"Yes. But let me tell you the story in order."

"Well, after I went over the side, Matthew and I struggled for control of my body. I was not sure how far away we needed to be from the boat to keep Matthew from taking control of someone else. I just knew that I was deep enough to drown. Matthew would not let me let go of the watch. I knew I had to do something quick, and that is when I remembered the bottle around my neck. I shoved the diving weight into my pocket to free up my other hand. I then yanked the bottle from around my neck, opened it and let the holy water swirl around me. I released the watch at the same time. I could feel Matthew leave my body to escape the holy water. The only place he could go was to return to the watch. I then let the gold cross fall into my hand and put it around my neck, thinking it would keep Matthew from trying to take control of me again."

"Pretty clever! What happened then?"

"By the time I got the bottle open and the cross around my neck, we had to have dropped to at least five hundred feet or more. By this time I had no idea how deep I was. I needed air fast, so I headed for the surface."

"But we never saw you come up."

"I know. I decided I didn't have enough air left to get to the surface in time. I remembered a documentary a few years ago about blue holes. It mentioned the walls are pitted and pockmarked with holes and caves. I guessed I was only fifty or sixty feet from the wall, so I headed in the direction I thought it was, hoping to find a cave with air. If I didn't, I was dead. It was pitch black at that depth, but I thought I saw darker patches in the wall that might be caves. It was so dark; it could have been my imagination. I was swimming so hard that I almost plowed into the wall. I started crawling up the wall, feeling for a cave. The first one I found didn't have any air at all. It felt like my lungs were about to explode. I pulled myself out of the cave and discovered one above it. Inside was a small shelf and an air pocket. I pulled myself onto it and collapsed from exhaustion. I'm not sure how long I was in there."

Barbara smiled, excited. "Mike, when you were in the water, we all gathered around while Captain Anthony said a prayer for you."

"Really?"

"Yes! You know what I think?"

"Uh-uh."

"I think God was watching over you."

"Maybe he was."

"So how did you get back to shore?"

"Oh, I nearly forgot! The pocket of air was not very big and I did not want to press my luck. Also, it was cold and I worried about hypothermia. I took several breaths and headed up the side of the wall. I managed to find more small caves with air, which also helped minimize the bends. After my strength returned I swam to the surface and saw the boat was gone. I floated for a while and was fortunate to be able to flag down some fishermen. By this time I was in pretty bad shape, so they took me to the hospital. I passed out and didn't wake up for several days. That's why I didn't come back until now."

Mike's voice softened, "I'm sorry for putting you through all of this. You must have been worried to death."

"You have no idea! I'm just glad everything worked out the way it did and you're here with me now."

"Me too!" he said, holding her tight and nuzzling her hair. "Me too!!!"

*   *   *

A week after they had disposed of the watch, Mike wrote a report to the Jamaican National Trust. In it he listed the artifacts found, their condition, and noted it would be a great travesty if the harbor were to be dredged for commercial purposes. When he had finished, Mike carried the report to the dive shack to let Barbara read it.

She studied the paper. "It reads well, but you misspelled archaeological."

Mike leaned over to see. "Where?"

She laughed at his reaction. "I was only kidding."

He reached for the paper, and she pulled it away. "Uh—uh. I'm not finished with it yet."

She read some more and became serious. "This says you're leaving the excavation."

"Yes, it does. My job is through. Everything the Trust wanted to know is in that report."

"But, Mike, what are you going to do?"

"I have an offer to head the excavation of a Civil War wreck off the coast of North Carolina. I think they said it was a blockade-runner by the name of *Atlantis*. Maybe I'll work that for a while. I thought you might want to come with me."

Barbara shook her head in frustration. "Oh, I knew you'd come up with something like this now."

"So what's the problem?"

"Mr. Wilkens asked if I could stay on here and help the new team of divers. I told him I'd think about it. He anticipates a much larger operation next year."

"I see. What are you going to tell him?"

"Well, I've worked hard to get this position. It means a great deal to me. But so do you."

Mike removed a gold box from his pocket and opened it. "Maybe this will help you decide. Barbara Anderson, will you do me the honor of becoming my wife?"

Barbara took the box with trembling hands. "Oh, Mike, the ring is beautiful! Yes, I'll marry you! A thousand times yes!" she said tearfully and flung her arms around Mike.

THE END

Richard H. Triebe